FLAWED PERFECTION

A Love Story

R. M. BURGESS

PAGE PUBLISHING, INC.
New York, NY

First originally published by Page Publishing, Inc. 2019

Cover painting by Ekaterina Turkina

ISBN 978-1-64544-848-8 (Paperback)
ISBN 978-1-64544-847-1 (Digital)

Printed in the United States of America

Also by R. M. Burgess

The Chronicles of New Eartha

- *The Chess Players of Brosen*
- *The Empire of the Zon*
- *The Eclipse of the Zon – First Tremors*
- *The Eclipse of the Zon – Rising Dark*

R. M. Burgess author site:

https://www.amazon.com/R.M.-Burgess/e/B00EYXDSSO/

PREFACE

The bards delight in singing us sad songs of unrequited love and fickle or faithless lovers, of the chasms that separate them and cause broken hearts. This is a love story, so it has elements of all of these. It is the story of a love grows in spite of the intentions of the two protagonists. A pair of opposites drawn together through a common professional interest, but who each find something more to appreciate in the other.

Human relationships are inherently unpredictable, asymmetric, and unstable. They can arise in the least likely situations, their true nature lurking in the subconscious, never consciously recognized until some event, trivial, or dramatic releases them into the open. Most relationships are purely instrumental, but some morph into something far more tender. Others not. Is it the context, the object, or the person? Are some of us more capable of a great love than others?

James Hancock is a sensible, rational man, a banker who has always made the "right" choices. He rises from poverty on the basis of his geeky, intellectual acumen. Like most successful people, he's had a single-minded focus on achieving what he thinks he wants—wealth, status, the perfect family for the Christmas cards. After a quarter century of striving, he's achieved all of his youthful goals, and he's satisfied with his life. He's followed the straight and narrow. It's led him to the life he dreamed of, so he must be happy, right? But he's never asked himself that question. How many of us do?

As with all my novels, I have many people to thank. Ekaterina Turkina's art graces the front cover. Agnieszka Nowinska, Sarfaraz Shroff, Noemi Sinkovics, and Helene Tenzer critiqued the various drafts, and some of them were pretty rough, so I am grateful for their patience and time. Alex Berman worked with me to make the banking scenes as realistic as possible. Marcelo Cano-Kollmann helped me with the Argentinian scene, including the tango. All of my test readers helped me turn what was a very raw draft into something better. But most of all, they gave me the confidence to take my story to a wider audience—to you.

R. M. Burgess (Philadelphia, 2018)

TABLE OF CONTENTS

PROLOGUE
FANTASY

What is fantasy but an imagined reality?

1

I t all began with Julia. She was the daughter of my old friend and mentor, Henry Pierce, who'd long since moved south to run a bank in Atlanta, and was now retired. When I received the innocent email from Henry, I had no idea that his daughter would set in train a series of events that would turn my life upside down. He said that Julia had just accepted a position at my bank and needed a place to stay in the city—could I help? We had a one-bedroom condo in the city, a *pied-à-terre*. After checking with my wife, Dolores, I emailed Henry that we would be happy to let Julia use it till she found a place of her own. Julia responded, and Dolores arranged everything with her.

Well, perhaps I should back up a bit. I was the Head of Fixed-Income Trading and Managing Director of a major bank. I served on several corporate boards and was a trustee of the city's symphony and natural history museum. Dolores was a high school teacher. She was active on the hospital board and managed the volunteers for the county library. We were proud to be pillars of our local community.

Julia arrived when I was on a business trip to Europe. So the first thing I saw of her was the car with California plates in the driveway when I got out of my taxi from the airport on my return. I went inside the house and found Dolores sitting with our guest. She had just arrived in town and had come to pick up the keys to our condo.

My first reaction was surprise. My friend Henry had never been a particularly good-looking fellow, but his daughter Julia was incredibly pretty. She had a lovely heart-shaped face with brown eyes and the creamy smooth white complexion that Southern girls are known for. She had very straight shiny dark-brown hair that cascaded down to the middle of her back. She wore a short black skirt, a black and white crop top, and very high-heeled thong sandals. She had on a broad strap necklace with a lyre pendant and hoop earrings.

"Hello, I'm Julia Pierce," she said, advancing and offering me her hand. She had a charming Southern accent with just a little lilt. "It's pronounced 'purse' as in a lady's purse."

Of course, I'd known her father for years, so I knew this.

"I'm James Hancock," I said, shaking her hand.

She surprised me by giving me a spontaneous hug, rubbing herself against me rather more than courtesy demanded. I was acutely conscious of Dolores's presence and held her shoulders gingerly in response.

"I'm a huggy kind of girl, Mr. Hancock," she said. "Especially with people I like. I've already told Mrs. Hancock. I hope you don't mind."

"No, of course not," I said.

"I remember the last time we met like it was yesterday, Mr. Hancock. My family visited you when I was fourteen. I babysat Nathan and Heather, and you helped me so much with my summer math assignments. Mrs. Hancock and I were just reminiscing about it."

"Yes," said Dolores. "That was a lovely visit. The weather cooperated that summer, and we spent a lot of time outdoors, barbecuing. I remember your father showed Jim everything he was doing wrong at the barbecue grill."

"We had wonderful times walking all the lovely trails around here," said Julia. "I want to thank you both again for allowing me to use your place in the city. It is so very kind of you."

"It's no trouble at all," I said. "How's your father?"

"He's well, Mr. Hancock, and sends his best," she replied.

We chatted in the kitchen for a short while, and I learned that Julia had worked in retail banking for several years on the West Coast. She had been in loans administration while completing her CFA qualifications. After an appropriate period of time, Julia excused herself, saying she had to get to bed and be ready for work the next day. Dolores got the keys and explained the access and features of our condo building.

"I've left a folder on the kitchen table with detailed information," said Dolores. "But call me if you need anything. My cell is in the folder."

"Come by my office when you get in tomorrow morning," I said. "I'll walk you around and introduce you."

Once we were alone, I had a quick bite to eat, and Dolores filled me in with some more details. In her correspondence with Julia's mother Sarah, Dolores had learned that she had skipped two years of high school through an accelerated program and AP credits. She had been a straight A student in college and graduated at twenty. Sarah assured Dolores that Julia did not party and was very serious about her work.

"She sounds like she's twenty-eight, going on fifty," I joked as Dolores and I walked upstairs.

"Maybe she has a hidden wild side," said Dolores. "Didn't you see the lyre tattooed on her ankle?"

"A lyre?"

"Alpha Chi Omega. She's a sorority girl."

*   *   *

2

Dolores and I met in college. She was a year behind me. I got her pregnant when she was a senior, and we were married immediately after she graduated. She was a wonderful wife in every way. She was very supportive of my career and an excellent mother to our two children. She spent endless hours with them through the difficult years of middle school, high school, and college, when I was a bit of a standoffish father. Thanks to her, they'd both graduated from prestigious universities. Our son was working in a small artificial intelligence start-up, and our daughter was working pro bono for a medical charity. At forty-eight and forty-seven, we were empty nesters with a twenty-five year old son and a twenty-four year old daughter.

Dolores was a very businesslike, sensible woman, and quite attractive, but she was not particularly warm. She was not tactile and did not enjoy physical touching. We'd had wild, hormone-fueled sex as teenagers and in our early twenties. But after the children were born, her interest in sex became increasingly dutiful. Eventually, by our thirties, she endured rather than enjoyed our physical coupling. While she met her conjugal obligations, she told me quite frankly that she was only doing it to service my physical needs. Our sex life degenerated to a once-a-week affair, usually on weekends. Even then, it only took place if I did elaborate planning to ensure it was not too early (when she would be reading or watching television) and not too late (when she would be too sleepy). She never wanted the light on and was always in a hurry to "get it over with." In the last few years, we sometimes went months without sex. I'm embarrassed to admit that there were times when I resorted to online pornography.

*   *   *

3

Julia came to my corner office bright and early the next day. She walked down the picture windows along the two walls, taking in the views of the Hudson and the street far below. She wore a black business suit with a modest knee-length skirt.

"I'm so happy to be here, Mr. Hancock," she said.

She gave me another unprompted hug with enough intimacy and duration to make me uncomfortable. My professional instinct was to push her away, but I allowed her to take her time releasing me. I was relieved when she finally did. Or was I? I was not sure.

"I just *know* I'm going to enjoy working for you," she said.

She was going to be working for someone significantly lower in the corporate hierarchy than me, but it seemed churlish to mention that. I walked her around and introduced her to all the analysts. Then I walked her down to the trading floor and introduced her with the chief of trading, asking him to get her set up.

"Come by my office about noon," I said. "Since it's your first day, I'll take you to lunch."

Thereafter, I saw Julia almost every day. She made it a habit to come by my office early in the morning and discuss her work from the previous day. I critiqued what she had done and offered her suggestions. She always rewarded me with a hug, sometimes a kiss on the cheek.

She also worked very hard, staying later than most of the other traders. On days when it got too late to go home for dinner with Dolores, Julia and I sometimes had dinner in the city together. I discovered that she kept several pairs of shoes in her cubicle. She always wore very tall, spiky heels for her evenings with me. She would ask to hang on my arm as the city sidewalks were "too rough." She leaned on me like we were on a date and always seemed to get us seated in a booth or on a bench so she could sit close to me. Over time, I got used to her physical closeness. It was hard to avoid feeling smug when I saw the looks of envy or respect in the eyes of other men when they saw Julia on my arm. Of course, they were assuming a relationship that did not exist, but I was happy for them to reach that conclusion.

I know that I should have stopped it, but I confess that I could not resist the admiring company of such an attractive young woman. While her mathematical abilities were no better than the average trader and her approach was mechanical rather than theoretical, she was bright enough to understand my complex trading strategies. As the days stretched into weeks, her compliments about my knowledge and strategies were subtle enough to convince me that they were genuine and not mere flattery.

It was such a contrast to my conversations with Dolores, who judged everything I said or did to be stupid, wrong, or both. I felt things were perfect, for I was not cheating on my wife but enjoying all the external benefits of having a gorgeous, young mistress. I rationalized it, arguing to myself that I would help any of the bank's traders exactly as I was helping Julia. I was so confident of the blamelessness of my position that I was quite open with Dolores. I always called her, inviting her to join Julia and me for dinner. She invariably declined, for Dolores hated coming into the city.

*   *   *

4

I was quite a serious runner and ran with a marathon club in the city every Saturday. The club met in the largest city park at eight in the morning. Usually, about twenty to thirty runners showed up and ran the first few miles together, thereafter, breaking up into smaller groups that ran different speeds and different distances. I usually ran at least ten miles with one of the faster groups. When I was training for a marathon, I often ran much longer than that.

About a month after Julia started working at the bank, I went for my usual club long run. On my return, I was walking on the grass in the park, cooling down, when I saw Julia running toward me. She was wearing neon yellow Nike sports bra, matching shorts, and yellow Nike running shoes. Her running socks were low rise, so I saw the pink and green lyre tattooed on her right ankle. It was a hot, muggy day, and she was covered with sweat.

"Well!" I said. "I didn't know you were a runner. I'd have invited you to run with my club."

"Oh, I barely run at all, Mr. Hancock," she said. "I just run a bit around the park, very slow. I couldn't possibly run with your club."

"Would you like a drink?" I asked.

"Sure, Mr. Hancock." She linked her arm in mine as we walked toward a refreshment stand. There were a few runners from my club still stretching, and I introduced Julia to everyone as a coworker at the bank. Then we took our soft drinks to lie on the grass in the shade.

"Do you mind if I put my head on your stomach, Mr. Hancock?" she asked.

We lay in the grass and chatted for over an hour before I dropped Julia back at our condo and drove home. Dolores was out, and the big house was quiet. I could not get the picture of Julia's sweat-covered body in her skimpy running outfit out of my mind.

* * *

5

As I expected, under my tutelage, Julia got the hang of running complex trades very quickly. With the contacts and trades I sent her way, she was soon showing a great bottom line. The chief of trading loved her work, and she got her own desk in less than two months. She was on the fast track.

"Where did you find this girl, Jim?" the chief of trading said to me a month after Julia started running trades under my guidance. "She's leaving all the boys in the dust!"

"I know her father," I said.

"Those boys at the trading desks have filthy mouths, but she's got them acting like choirboys around her. How does she do it?"

"Southern charm," I said, "and double digit margins."

He walked away, shaking his head.

* * *

6

I realized that my relationship with Julia was dangerous. While I enjoyed spending time with her, as well as the physical closeness that she lavished on me, I recognized she was a strong and consistent temptation. I often wondered what would happen if I were to respond to her apparent invitations. I was very fond of her, but I knew that I did not want to go down that road. I was content with the idea that an intelligent, highly desirable young woman wanted me. I thought of Julia as an authentic and direct person, as my grand passion, a love that could have been but wasn't.

So I got her transferred to London. I kept tabs on her and made sure it was known that she had a powerful sponsor in the rough and tumble world of fast-paced, high-pressure bond trading. Once she found her feet, she did very well and rapidly became one of the bank's best performing Eurobond traders.

I still sent trades to her desk—even though I knew that she did not need them. She was still the well-brought-up Southern girl that she had always been. I received an old-fashioned note in the mail after each trade I sent her way, with a few lines expressing her gratitude. I enjoyed receiving these missives in her neat, rounded handwriting, and perhaps that was why I sent the trades to her.

Two years went by, and then I heard through the office grapevine that she was engaged to a German equity trader that she met in London. A few months later, I got an invitation to her wedding down in Atlanta. I showed it to Dolores, but she said, "Georgia in June! I'm not going down there in that heat. We barely know the girl."

CHAPTER I

REALITY

1

I saw Julia every other month at bank meetings in London. She had not changed and still treated me with the same closeness as when we first met. My interest in her remained strong. I kept a detailed track of her activities in the bank and followed her on social media. Two years after her marriage, four years after I sent her to London, she had a baby with her German husband, Gunter von Hakenberg, a boy named Maximilian. I saw the photo album on her social media account, full of smiling family, including her father, my old friend Henry Pierce.

While Julia was extremely successful as a Eurobond trader, I knew from general finance community gossip that her husband's performance as an equity trader was not going nearly as well. In fact, von Hakenberg had been in the bottom 10 percent of traders at his

German bank for several quarters now. This was a rather damning indictment since his bank's traders as a whole were not doing that well.

*   *   *

2

A month after Julia's son was born, the chief of our bank's Eurobond trading desk was hired away by a competitor. Sheridan Logan Baldwin III, the bank president, called me in to discuss a replacement. I walked into his corner suite and saw my name on his appointments viewscreen behind his secretary's head, James Hancock, 9:30 a.m. I knocked and went in, and he waved me to a seat.

"Well, Jim," said the president, who went by Logan, "Eurobonds have been a major contributor to our bottom line these last few years. This is a key position, and Gary leaving us like this is a huge blow. Who do you have in mind for a replacement? You'll have to hire someone from the outside, won't you? Our Eurobond team in London has been doing well, but they're awfully young and green."

"They're young, I'll give you that," I said. "But they're quite experienced now. Gary didn't do much. He simply sat in his office, let them rack up the numbers, and came here to headquarters every quarter to take the credit."

"Really? Who do you have in mind?"

"Well," I looked out of the picture windows of his downtown corner suite, which commanded an excellent view of both the city's rivers. "Julia Pierce has the best numbers."

"Pierce!" He drummed his fingers on his desk. "She's a bright girl. I'll grant you. She's also hot as hell. But that's just the point—will she be taken seriously?"

"She's handled the biggest bond deals we've done," I said. "Even the Saudis like dealing with her, despite the fact that she won't wear a headscarf. And you know how fussy they are about that. And the Japanese, too, misogynistic and macho as they are."

"The Japanese always want us to provide them with high-class hookers," Logan said garrulously.

"Well, I don't know if Julia does that. But she keeps them happy."

"I like Julia, so I'll support you. But I want you to go to London and handle the transition. Make sure that things are running smoothly under her before you return."

"How long are we talking?" I asked.

"I don't know, Jim," said Logan. "When it looks stable, you can come home."

"I'm a married man, Logan. I can't just go to London on an open-ended assignment. What about the rest of my global responsibilities?"

"Just move your global office to London, Jim, and take Dolores with you. She's earned some time off, hasn't she?"

* * *

3

"It's a great opportunity, Doll," I said to Dolores. "You'll have a great time. We'll be based in London, but all of Europe is just an hour away—and you'll have the freedom to travel."

"You've never taken my career seriously, Jim," Dolores sniffed. "I can't just drop everything and leave for Europe."

"I'm not asking you to give up your career," I said. "Can't you just take a year's sabbatical or something?"

I talked, I begged, I pleaded. But nothing got through to Dolores.

"Just go by yourself," she said. "I'm sure that's what you would prefer anyway."

"If I wanted to go by myself, why would I be begging you to come with me?" I asked.

"You're just saying that," she said. "But you don't really want me to come."

On my last night in town, I prepared very carefully. I lit some thick aromatic candles, turned down the lights, and pulled the sheets back tastefully in our bedroom. When Dolores came up after dinner, I was waiting with a bottle of champagne in a silver ice bucket by the bed.

"I really don't want to drink," she said immediately. "It's a weeknight."

"I thought we could make love," I said. "It will be some time before we are together again."

"I'd rather read my book," she said before going to her boudoir to change.

She slid into bed and picked up her book from the nightstand. I gave up. After she put out the lights, I got out of bed, walked down the corridor to the upstairs bathroom that I used, and took a cold shower.

*   *   *

4

I arrived in Heathrow with just carry-on bags. The rest of my luggage was arriving later by cargo, and my staff was slated to join me over the coming month. I sailed through the channel for first-class passengers. Mildred, my ever efficient assistant told me that I would be met at the airport, so I looked around for one of the uniformed chauffeurs that the bank always used. I was surprised when I felt my elbow touched and looked around, for chauffeurs *never* did that.

It was Julia. She wore a classic black Chanel business suit with a short tight jacket worn over a white chiffon blouse. The skirt was knee-length but very tight and had a high slit. She had on black hose so dark that only careful observation enabled me to see the fishnet design. She had a white-gold choker necklace at her throat—it was in the form of a snake biting its own tail. Its small red ruby eyes winked in the lights of the terminal. Her long dark-brown hair was gathered in a severe, professional bun and she had on light, tasteful makeup.

I put out my hand, and she shook it awkwardly before giving me a hug. I could not resist holding her close, but she uncharacteristically pushed me away.

"I thought I would come to pick you up," she said, anticipating my question. "It will give us some time to talk privately on the drive to town. I have a suite for you at the Mayfair Hotel. I've also had our guest room prepared for you, if you would like to stay with us. We live around the corner, just off Berkeley Square."

"Thanks, Julia," I said as we walked toward the car park. "I'll stay at the hotel."

"Good," she said.

She led the way to the VIP parking apron just outside the terminal. As she walked, the slit in her skirt splayed open. It was high enough that I could see that she wore stockings, not pantyhose—and I caught glimpses of her black garters. She walked up to a brand new top-of-the-line Porsche 911, and the doors opened at her touch. I recognized the custom package from the beefy yellow brake calipers, which meant that it cost almost a quarter million.

"Fancy car," I said as I put my small carry-ons into the cramped area behind the seats. I had to lower myself nearly horizontal to get into the low-slung supercar. Julia got in, and the controls automatically moved to her settings and clicked her seat belt into place. She said, "Belt," and my seat belt moved over my body and settled into place.

"It's Gunter's car," she said as she pulled out into traffic. She got into the fast lane and onto the M4 motorway into London. "He's in Frankfurt till tomorrow, and my car is in the shop. So I borrowed it. He won't like it. He's very possessive about his things."

"What do you drive?" I asked.

"Just a little Audi A3," she said. "I don't know much about cars. I let Gunter take care of things like that."

One wheel on this Porsche is worth more than your entire car, I thought. *With his pathetic performance and your fat bonuses, your money is paying for this.*

"I'll drop you off at your hotel. You can take the rest of the day to shower, nap, and freshen up. I've arranged your first meeting with my group at four."

"Good," I said. "Do you have a busy day?"

"Yes, very busy. If you need anything, call my amazing assistant, Roxy Reid. She's like the Harrod's buying agent. Ask and she'll get it for you, from a latte to an elephant."

"An elephant!" I said. "Just what I always wanted."

"I'm not kidding. The Sumitomo Bank guys from Tokyo were here last week—you know they always have pretty bizarre demands. But they were all singing Roxy's praises at the signing ceremony."

"How'd you get them to sign?" I asked, curious.

"I leave the details of the entertainment to Roxy," said Julia evasively. "I don't ask her how she does it, and she doesn't tell me. You can ask her if you want."

"Tell me about it her."

"She was a bicycle messenger when I first met her. I quickly started using her exclusively because she was so dependable and never made excuses. Morning, evening, nights, all hours, all weathers. I'd message her, and she'd be there in her Lycra and leather, helmet under her arm, ready to work. After a year or so, I asked her how much she made. I offered to double her pay, and she came to work for me the next day. She's been with me ever since, getting nice raises."

We were nearing the Chiswick Roundabout, where the M4 dumps into the Great West Road. Julia downshifted again, and the car switched into city mode. The engine note turned softer as it powered back.

"Roxy never graduated from high school. She had a tough east London upbringing—you know, lots of gangs and drugs. She's managed to get out of that quagmire, but she's retained all kinds of useful contacts that I prefer not to know about. She doesn't know anything about finance, but she's an amazing fixer. She gets things done."

"That's high praise coming from you. How old is she?"

"Maybe that's one of the reasons I like her so much," said Julia, pulling out and passing a taxi. "She's very young, barely twenty, I think—and she worships me."

"You must be her role model," I said.

"She's as different from me as one could possibly be. She's got a nose ring, rings on the tops of her earlobes, a belly button piercing, and a Lao Tzu quote in Chinese characters tattooed on her back—'The master acts without doing anything and teaches without saying anything.' She still wears leather to work with short tops that bare her midriff and display her belly button piercing. Sometimes it's a stud. Sometimes it's a ring."

"That can't go over well."

"No, it doesn't. The older traders hate her. The younger ones keep hitting on her and spread stories about her because she won't sleep with them. She's got a hot bod from all that biking. She still races bikes competitively."

"She's pretty, I take it," I said.

"Very," said Julia. "Would be even prettier if she didn't wear all that metal and streak her black hair with purple dye."

"Well, she seems to have good taste in men. Most of those young traders are scumbags."

"You must have been a young trader once," Julia said, teasing.

"I was married and did not hit on women at work," I said defensively.

"I was just baiting you," said Julia, patting my thigh. I reciprocated and placed my hand on her thigh, just at the hem of her skirt.

"Don't," she said, pushing my hand away.

I was surprised, for she'd always welcomed such mild touching in the past. She drove for a few more moments in silence.

"You're happy with how things are going?" I asked. "Marriage, baby?"

"Yes," she said. She did not elaborate and did not sound convincing. We were passing through Hammersmith now, and it had started to drizzle. The intelligent wipers began moving. I kept looking at her sharp profile, waiting for her to go on.

"Look, Mr. Hancock," she said, "I know you're unhappy in *your* marriage."

"I'm very happy," I responded automatically, and the conversation dried up.

We arrived at the hotel without incident, and Julia got out of the car as the bellboy insisted on taking my light carry-ons. She gave me another quick hug in the hotel portico. But she put her hands on my chest when I put my arms around her in return.

"If you need anything, call Roxy," she said before getting back into the car.

*   *   *

5

I went up to my suite, disappointed with the change in Julia's demeanor. I napped for a couple of hours, then rose, showered, and shaved. I pulled on one of the hotel's fluffy robes, feeling the luxurious, soft material on my skin. I ordered up a pot of coffee from room service. It came within minutes, symptomatic of the hotel's excellent service. I skimmed the financial pages on my laptop as I sipped my coffee, then picked up my phone. There was one unread text. It was from Julia with Roxy's number.

I looked at my watch. It was almost ten. Still six hours before my meeting at four. I called Roxy.

"Yes." The accent on the phone was working-class British, discernable from that single word.

"James Hancock," I said. "I'd like to talk to Ms. Roxy Reid."

"This is Roxy."

"Ms. Reid, I'd like to go over the materials for my four o'clock meeting. Could you email them to me, please?"

"Certainly, Mr. Hancock. Please call me Roxy. It gives me the willies when you call me Ms. Reid. Like I'm in the dock for murder or somethin'." There was a pause, and I was about to give her my email address when she went on. "If you like, I can bring *all* the data over on one of the bank laptops."

"That's a good idea, Roxy. I'm in Suite 402."

She arrived much sooner than I expected—in under thirty minutes—so I was still in the hotel robe when she knocked on the door. I debated asking her to wait for me downstairs, decided against it, and opened the door.

Roxy was elfin, barely over five feet tall. The top of her head did not reach my shoulder, even though she was wearing clunky Kevlar-braced knee-high motorcycle boots. She had a motorcycle helmet with a full visor under her arm and wore a leather-Kevlar riding jacket with heavy metal zippers. She had on a leather skirt that came to mid-thigh, and there was a leather messenger bag over her back on a cross-strap. She had a steel-studded leather choker around her neck that looked like a dog collar and wore fingerless leather-Lycra gloves. Her nose ring and the rings on her ears were a mix of silver and brass.

Every item from her helmet to her boots was black. Her hair was jet black as well with purple streaks. It was thick, very straight, and cut in a short bob. All that black made her very white skin look even paler and her blue eyes even brighter. Julia was right. Even with her Goth turnout and her aggressive manner, she was a beauty, a pocket Venus. Her nose was thin and aquiline, and her facial structure was very delicate.

She was drenched, and puddles rapidly formed on the floor under her. Her helmet had kept her hair dry, but the rest of her was soaking wet.

"Hello, Mr. Hancock," she said, pushing past me and entering the suite without waiting for me to invite her in. "It's pissing it down out there. Nearly got taken out by a bus on my way here."

She unzipped her jacket and threw it on one of the chintz, overstuffed chairs in the suite. Then she threw her wet messenger bag on the big antique wooden office desk that dominated the living room of the suite. She pulled off her motorcycle boots one at a time and threw them in front of one of the radiators.

She wore a black silk sleeveless top and black fishnet stockings. Her jacket had kept the top dry, but her stockings were wet above her boot line. The top was thin and tight, and she had great looking legs under her fishnet stockings. Julia was right again. She had an incredibly hot body.

"Do you have another of those robes, Mr. Hancock? It would be great to dry my knickers and stockings before we have to go back to the office."

"Your panties, ah, I mean, your knickers are wet, are they?" I asked.

"Yes, Mr. Hancock," she said impatiently. "That's what I said."

"There's another robe in the bathroom."

She disappeared into the bathroom and came out, belting a matching robe around her narrow waist. It looked a lot better on her than on me, even though it came down to her ankles. She went to her leather messenger bag and pulled out a sleek laptop. She set it up on the office desk and sat down in one of the swivel chairs.

"I've got all the data pertaining to the meeting agenda here, Mr. Hancock."

"You'll go over it with me?" I asked, surprised. Julia had specifically mentioned that Roxy knew nothing about finance.

"If it's okay with you," Roxy said.

"Yes, yes," I said. "Thank you."

I pulled up the matching swivel chair and sat down next to her. Shoeless, in matching robes, we looked like a couple. She showed me the bond portfolios held in London, arranged by country, by instrument, and by various other groupings. She made a few remarks about the portfolios as she pulled them up that indicated that she understood them. This was quite impressive, as some of them were quite complex. However, after my initial surprise at her depth of knowledge, I was only half listening. The incongruous circumstances made it hard for me to concentrate. I knew that I was missing much of the detail. I tried to at least retain the gist of what she was saying to ensure that I did not make a fool of myself at the meeting.

I excused myself after half an hour and went to use the restroom. My eyes were drawn to her leather skirt, panties, and stockings that she had draped on the towel rail to dry. I was safely behind the locked bathroom door, so I guiltily allowed my imagination to run free for a moment. I flushed the toilet and returned to seat myself in my swivel chair by her side. I kept both my hands in my lap, for her physical proximity and attire were quite distracting.

She picked up where she had left off, and I again concentrated on retaining the bare essentials of what she was telling me. Finally, at the end of an hour, she sat back saying, "Well, that's about it, Mr. Hancock. I hope I've given you a complete picture of our Eurobond value at risk."

"Yes, thank you, Roxy," I said. "Excellent summary."

"What do you think of our position in Singapore dollar instruments?"

I couldn't remember anything about Singapore, but I assumed I must have missed it.

"Good, good," I said. "Of course, I'll have to see all the details in the meeting today to be certain."

"Liar," she said, smiling. "You weren't paying attention, were you? We don't have any holdings in Singapore dollars at the moment."

"We don't?"

"Mr. Hancock," said Roxy, "I think I know where your mind is."

"No, no," I said. Her meaning was clear from her tone, and alarm seeped into my voice. "Thank you for coming, Roxy. You can return to the office now...I'll see you at the meeting."

She looked as calm as I was flustered. She reached forward, and her hand darted under mine in my lap and found the seam in my robe. She was too quick for me. Before I could stop her, I felt the coldness of the rings she wore on three of her fingers.

"I was right, wasn't I, Mr. Hancock?"

"There's no regulation against it!" I cried. "I've not violated bank policy! I've done nothing illegal. I will report you for sexual harassment."

She started laughing, but she did not release me.

"Report me for sexual harassment! Go ahead. I can see it on the news now—Fifteen stone fifty-something bank managing director harassed by eight stone twenty-year-old admin assistant."

She laughed again. It was genuine mirth, for I could not discern anything malicious. I was still totally unnerved and did not under-stand her right away.

"Stone?" I muttered. "I don't get it."

"I'm one hundred ten pounds," she translated. "You're about two ten or nearly twice my weight. Do you think anyone will believe that I harassed you?"

Her fingers moved gently.

"Roxy!" I cried. "Don't do that! Please!"

She did the opposite, increasing her tempo. I grasped her wrist with both my hands, but she was strong for a small girl. I could see the powerful muscles of her forearm bunch as she continued her motion against the pressure of both my hands. She put her other hand on my cheek.

"Shhh," she whispered. Her harsh working-class accent grated on my ears. "Just relax, Mr. Hancock. You want this. You know you do. What are you worried about?"

"You're right," I said, a note of misery entering my voice. "No one will believe that I didn't sexually harass you. I've worked hard all my life, Roxy. Why are you doing this to me?"

"Shhh," she whispered again. "I don't want to destroy you, Mr. Hancock."

"Are you recording this?"

"No. Do you want me to?"

"No! No! Of course not!" I cried.

"Don't upset yourself, Mr. Hancock."

I kept my hold on her wrist with both my hands, but I recognized that the damage was done. I'd received her in my suite, naked under my robe. That was evidence enough for any investigating committee. She could destroy me if she chose. I closed my eyes and willed myself to relax. Once she sensed this, she brushed my lips with hers. I smelled mint and coffee on her breath.

She knew what she was doing, and in less than a minute, she had me gasping for breath. I sagged back onto the old desk and put my head on one of my arms. I realized that there was a thin line of drool leaking out of the side of my mouth, and I quickly wiped it away. As the high slowly dissipated, I sat up.

Roxy was sitting on the edge of her chair, hands on her thighs, her expression playful.

"Naughty, naughty, Mr. Hancock," she said, wagging a finger. "You already wanked in the bathroom, didn't you?"

"No, no," I said, but I sounded unconvincing, even to myself.

She patted my cheek again.

"Don't lie, Mr. Hancock."

"What do you want, Roxy?" I asked tiredly. "Money? I'll give you what I have. I can get more."

"Do you think I'd jerk you off for money, Mr. Hancock?" she said, showing anger for the first time. "Do you think I'm a whore?"

"I don't know what to think, Roxy," I said. My dejection seemed to get through to her, and she smiled.

She stood up and paced around the room with smooth, feline grace.

"I grew up in a tough neighborhood, Mr. Hancock. Not quite as bad as your American ghettos but bad enough. Lots of violence, the occasional killing. The local hierarchy was all in the gangs, and their power was based on the money they made running drugs. I learned very young that the only way for a woman to survive was to find a powerful protector and give him what he wanted in exchange for a safe position in the hierarchy."

"Is that what you did?"

"Yes. The details are not important, but I latched onto a powerful man, and I eventually became his girlfriend. I rode my bicycle, did my legitimate messenger job, and gave him what he wanted. Sometimes, Nick made me run drugs for him, but that was rare because I was good at managing him."

"Did you sleep with him?"

"You're either naive or stupid, Mr. Hancock," she said. "I'm going with naive because I know you're not stupid. How do you think I managed him?"

"How old were you?"

"I grew up fast, Mr. Hancock."

"So this gang boss—Nick—is he still your boyfriend?"

"No, Mr. Hancock. When I came to work for Julia, I broke up with Nick and moved to west London."

"How did this Nick take it?"

"It wasn't like Nick was faithful to me. I was his number one girl, but he had plenty of others. In a way, he was glad to see me go. I gave him too much lip and was always beating up other girls that slept with him."

"Beating up other girls," I said, shaking my head. I'd never met anyone remotely like Roxy. "I'm impressed with your rise from poverty, Roxy, but—"

"You're wondering what this has to do with you." She ran her fingers through her hair, broadening out the purple streaks. "I've only been at the bank a short time, Mr. Hancock. But long enough to see that it's not much different from where I grew up."

"That's ridiculous!" I exclaimed.

"Is it? Julia's one of the youngest lead traders on the Eurobond desk, yet her team runs the biggest trades. And now she's slated to become the chief of the desk. In the short time I've been there, I've seen women traders with much fancier degrees than her, and much more experience, come and go. They get their trades stolen by the 'boys club,' then leave after a few months for showing no results. It's every bit as cutthroat as where I grew up, Mr. Hancock. A young woman needs a protector."

"Really?"

"Don't play dumb with me, Mr. Hancock. Everyone knows that you're Julia's protector."

"Everyone?" I asked. "Do they think that I sleep with—"

"Yes," Roxy said firmly.

"But she's married!"

"We all see the trades you send to her personally, Mr. Hancock. The message to everyone here is clear—she's my girl. Don't mess with her."

"Roxy, you must believe me. There is nothing between Julia and me."

She crossed her arms over her breasts. Then she smiled.

"Have it your way, Mr. Hancock." She took her phone out of the robe pocket and looked at the time. "It's just coming up to eleven. We have over five hours till the meeting."

"What do you want, Roxy?" I asked again.

"Julia's got what she wanted. She's married. She's going to be chief of the Eurobond desk. Soon, she won't need you anymore. You're going to need a girl to take her place in your bed. I want to be that girl."

"Julia is very impressed with you, Roxy," I said. "She'll take care of you. You don't need me."

"I don't want to be Julia's assistant forever!" Roxy snapped, suddenly angry again. "'Roxy, get me a latte,' 'Roxy, arrange entertainment for our Japanese clients,' Roxy do this, Roxy do that. Julia will never let me become a trader. She wants to be the only cute thing on the Eurobond desk. She doesn't want competition."

"Julia is not like that," I said, shocked. "She's a sweet, honest, Southern girl. She always plays fair."

Roxy read my face like an open book.

"You're soft on her, aren't you," she said. Her powder blue eyes opened wide. "You're a romantic. Poor deluded Mr. Hancock. She's getting what she wants from you without even sleeping with you, isn't she?"

"I told you, she's married—"

"Look, Mr. Hancock," said Roxy, cutting me off, "I'm a girl from the gutter. I'm not respectable like Julia. But where I come from, we believe in straight barter, no subterfuge. I'll sleep with you, and in exchange, you'll help me get a financial qualification. And protect me from the sharks on the floor who'll try to steal my trades."

"But Julia—"

"Forget Julia," said Roxy brusquely. "She'll string you along and get what she wants out of you for another year or so. She's been building her network to reduce her dependence on you. Did you know that she has one-on-one dinner meetings with Logan Baldwin every time he passes through London? Once she doesn't need you anymore, it'll be 'Goodbye, Mr. Hancock.'"

This was a shock to me. I didn't know that Julia was spending time with Logan. The bank president was a notorious womanizer. Could Julia be sleeping with him? Logan's words at our meeting came back to me, "She's also hot as hell."

"And how are you any better?"

"I'm honest, Mr. Hancock. I'm telling you up front, it's just sex. I'm not trying to make you fall in love with me."

"You'll have to pass the exams to get your financial qualification, Roxy."

"I need you to help me study. To tell me what to read, be my tutor. I've studied your work, Mr. Hancock. You're the smartest man in the bank, a genius. Even Julia says so."

"Okay, Roxy," I said. "You're a clever girl. The way you described our value at risk showed me that. I'll tutor you. But you don't have to sleep with me."

"Mr. Hancock, I want to be your special girl, the one you think about all the time. That won't happen unless I sleep with you."

"You're a cynic, Roxy."

"Yes, I am," she agreed.

She dropped her phone on the desk by the computer. Then she dropped her robe. My mouth dropped open, and I did not have the awareness to close it. She had a dark-blue tattoo of barbed wire running from her left hip along her pelvic bone. She slowly undid her silk blouse, a button at a time. Her moves were so sensual that my mouth went dry. She let the blouse slide down her arms to fall on the floor.

She pulled me to my feet, spread my robe with her hands, and pushed my arms back till it slid off my naked body. I covered myself with my hands. Then she took one of my hands in hers and pulled it away from my feeble attempt at covering my nakedness. She led me to the suite's bedroom and to the wide bed. I saw the Chinese characters tattooed between her shoulder blades.

"Roxy," I said, ashamed. "I can't—"

"I know," she cooed. "We have time."

She slid under the covers, I followed, and we cuddled. When I hugged her small strong body to mine, I felt her cold metal against my skin. Roxy was like nothing in my experience.

After some time, I asked her, "Do you have a condom?"

"I'm clean, Mr. Hancock. And I'm on the pill."

With her in my arms, I accepted risks that my thinking mind would not have allowed. She rolled me on to my back and straddled me. My thinking mind shut down completely, overwhelmed by her sheer physicality. It was pleasure beyond anything in my limited experience. I thought I heard the sound of a door, but my mind was so focused on what Roxy was doing to me that it did not register.

Then, just as I approached the high point, over Roxy's shoulder, I saw Dolores in the doorway to the suite bedroom. She wore a dripping raincoat, and her sling purse hung from her shoulder. Her hair was damp from the rain. Her lips were compressed in a thin line, and she was staring at us with a fixed expression. It was physically impossible for me to stop now. My eyes locked with Dolores's. I let myself go.

* * *

6

Dolores still did not say a word and just stood there, looking like a thundercloud. Roxy recovered quickly, though her blue eyes were still bright in the afterglow of our lovemaking. She sensed Dolores's presence and twisted around. She gasped when she saw her.

"I thought you were serious when you said how much you wanted me to come to London with you," said Dolores, her voice dripping venom. "So I hopped on a plane just after you left, thinking I would surprise you. I guess the surprise is on me. What a fool I was! I should have trusted my instincts. I knew you never wanted me here."

"Doll," I said. "That's not true! I don't—"

"Don't say anything more, Jim," she said. "You're barely in London for a few hours, and you're already in bed with a young girl. She looks fifteen! Have you no shame? I should call the police."

I looked at Roxy with fresh eyes. Small and extremely fit, she looked younger than her twenty years. I could see why Dolores's guess of fifteen was not a bad one. But her mention of the police scared the hell out of me.

"She's of age, Doll!" I exclaimed hastily. "She's—"

"I'm twenty," Roxy interjected. "I'm older than I look."

"Doll, listen to me," I said. "I know this looks bad, but let me explain. I never wanted this to happen—"

"How do you do, Mrs. Hancock?" said Roxy, cutting me off smoothly. Now she moved off my lap. She moved out of the wide bed on her hands and knees with catlike fluidity and got to her feet. "I'm pleased to meet you, but I will leave you with your husband now." She turned back to me. "It's been a pleasure doing business with you, Mr. Hancock. Thank you for paying cash up front."

Roxy began to walk by Dolores to get her clothes. As she approached her, the difference was stark. Dolores was nearly six feet tall and towered over Roxy's waiflike stature. My wife did not move and remained barring the doorway.

"Ms...."

"The name is Fifi."

"Fifi, I'd like you to stay and hear me out. As a prostitute, I am sure you have had many such experiences in your line of work. Most of your—what to you call them?—johns, are married, are they not? Cheating on their wives?"

"Yes, most are," said Roxy, nodding.

"Even when he cheats, my husband has no imagination. He's always been a boring, uninteresting man. The only way he could get a young girl like you to spend time with him would be to pay her."

"I'm not sure about that, Mrs. Hancock."

"You would say that, wouldn't you? He's paying you. And you pretend to have orgasms to build up his ego. I heard you. But I know my husband. He's always been as boring in bed as he is out of it."

Roxy looked from Dolores to me and back again.

"Well, I have nothing further to do here," said Dolores. "I'll head back to the airport and change my ticket to go back home on the first available flight."

"Doll, don't do this!" I cried. "Let me explain! It's all my fault, but we can work this out. I need you—"

"No, Jim. This time, I've had it. I've been miserable with you for years. I gave you the best years of my life. I brought up our children. I was there for you when you were building your career. This is how you repay me." A few angry tears appeared in her eyes. It seemed to me that she was forcing them out. "It will be difficult, but I will have to tell the children how disgusting their father is. It's a mercy that they are adults. And I'll tell Logan and everyone at the bank what a miserable turd you are. You'll hear from my lawyers. I'm going to take everything from you, every penny."

She turned on her heel and left before I could get another word out. I heard the front door to the suite slam behind her.

* * *

7

There was moment of silence. Roxy came back and sat on the bed beside me. She leaned over to kiss me, but I pushed her away.

"Why did you tell Dolores that you're a prostitute, Roxy?" I asked.

"She's going to tell everyone at the bank," she replied. "Do you want it broadcasted that you were in bed with a twenty-year-old admin assistant? They'd definitely sack you for that."

"Thank you," I said, realizing the truth of what she said. Roxy was so much worldlier than me. I was impressed anew with her quick thinking.

"Will she divorce you?"

"I don't know. Probably."

"Will she get all your assets?"

"Almost certainly. They're all in her name anyway. I won't fight her. She deserves to get everything. She's been a perfect wife. She gave her whole life to me."

"You make her sound like a saint. I don't know much about your life, Mr. Hancock. But in the talk around the bank, your wife doesn't sound nearly that angelic."

"What?" I was genuinely surprised. "People talk about us at the bank?"

She laughed. It was a very nice laugh, a contrast to her harsh working-class accent.

"Mr. Hancock, you know your equations and how markets work. But you obviously don't know people." She ran her fingers through my ginger hair. "You're one of the most senior executives in the bank. Of course people talk about you. Especially after Julia arrived in London as your special girl."

"What do they say?"

"That your wife is cold. That she's often mean to you at official bank functions, constantly running you down in front of others and ridiculing you. That no one's ever seen her show any affection toward you. That you're always sending her flowers and chocolates from all over the world. That you always talk about how wonderful she is. That she drove you into Julia's arms."

I said nothing.

"I've just met your wife, Mr. Hancock, admittedly under rather stressful circumstances. But I'm a good judge of people. I had to be, growing up as I did. I think she's a cold calculating bitch."

"You're wrong, Roxy. Dolores is a supportive wife, who has been by my side for over twenty-five years. I've treated her shabbily, cheating on her like this."

"What do you want to do, rush after her to the airport? I could get you there before her."

"Yes!" I exclaimed. "I should go after her and beg her to stay with me. I know the city she's going to, and she wants to be on the first flight out. I could find out in no time."

"I'll do it," said Roxy.

She went to the other room and returned with her phone. She showed me the screen with the flight time and number. There was three o'clock departure. It was now just about noon.

"I should ask the hotel desk to get me a taxi—"

"No need, Mr. Hancock. I can get you there in under thirty minutes. She'll probably take the Heathrow Express from Paddington." She checked the time on her phone. "There's no way she'll make it to ticketing before one thirty. So we have at least an hour."

"Why are you doing all this for me?"

"I told you," said Roxy patiently, "you're my meal ticket. My way to a career in banking. I need you. So I have to protect you, even from yourself."

Roxy slid into bed with me again, snuggling up to me, and burying my face in her hair. Her shampoo had a faint smell of oranges. Her young body was enticing, but I disengaged myself from her, got out of bed, and retrieved my robe.

"Roxy, I'm going to beg Dolores to stay with me. I'm not going to have sex with you again."

"She'll never know," said Roxy.

"I'll know," I said. "I've already been disgusting, a slave to my desires."

"Don't be so hard on yourself, Mr. Hancock," said Roxy cheerfully. "All men are."

"I was faithful to Dolores for over twenty-five years," I said stubbornly.

"But were you happy?"

I looked at her with surprise. I didn't want to answer her question and let it hang. I realized I was quite thirsty. I opened one of the water bottles from the bedside table, drank deeply, and set it back down.

"Do you have a boyfriend now, Roxy?" I asked with sudden curiosity.

"Why do you ask?"

"I wondered if you are cheating on someone too."

"No," she said. "After I started with the bank and broke up with Nick, I only met one bloke I thought I might like. Derek is one of Julia's analysts and seemed sweet. We went out for dinner and had a right nice chat. But once he got me in his bedroom, he turned out to be right wanker. He wanted to tie me up and spank me, and when I said no, he grabbed me and tried to force me."

"What a disgusting brute!" I said, shocked. "What did you do?"

"Derek is a gorilla," she said. "Even bigger than you. He thought he would have an easy time handling me since I'm little. But he's just a soft middle-class bloke. He had no idea how to deal with a girl like me."

I was agape. She laughed at me and kissed me.

"I stamped on his foot with my heel and got free. Then I got me switchblade and brass knuckles out of me bag and told him that if he tried to stop me leaving, I'd beat his face in and cut his dick off."

Her accent got stronger as she got into storytelling, and I had to listen attentively to understand her.

"Of course, he came into the bank the next day and told all his mates that he'd fucked me. Now all of them try their luck with me every day. It was huge mistake to go out with that bloke."

"You carry a switchblade and brass knuckles in your purse?"

She looked at me like I was being dense again.

"Mr. Hancock, I used to be the girlfriend of one of the biggest drug dealers in London."

"So now you live alone?"

"Not exactly alone. I have Alfie."

"Who's Alfie?"

"My Great Dane."

"You have a Great Dane?" I exclaimed.

"Yes," she said. "One of Nick's upper-class clients gave him this purebred Great Dane puppy as a token of appreciation. But Nick didn't want it, so he gave it to me."

"It must be very difficult to keep such a big dog in the city."

"I have a dog service that I trust. They feed and walk him when I'm at work. Alfie is dear. They love him like I do. He sleeps in my bed with me. He licks me all over. You'll have to come over and spend the night at my place sometime. He'll lie in and warm both of us."

"That's not going to happen," I said firmly. "We'd better get showers if we're going to get to the airport on time. You can go first."

* * *

8

"Have you ridden on a motorbike before, Mr. Hancock?" Roxy asked as we exited the elevator into the underground car park.

"I had one when I was in college," I replied. "But not since then. And I never rode on the back."

"Well, you know how to lean then," she said. "Just hang on to me. We'll be fine."

She wore her black leathers and carried her high-tech helmet under one arm with her messenger bag slung over her shoulder. It was a short walk to the two-wheeler parking stripes. She lifted her motorbike off its kickstand and straddled it. It was a Ducati super-bike in candy apple red. I'm not an expert on motorbikes, but I knew it was very, very fast machine with a top speed of over 150 miles per hour.

"Put the other helmet on, Mr. Hancock," she said, pointing to a matching helmet locked to a bracket by the rear seat. She released the helmet lock when she unlocked the bike, and I cradled it in my hands before putting it on.

It was jet black and incredibly light, made of Kevlar and carbon fiber. It looked like a space helmet and felt like one when I put it on.

"The chin strap snaps on automatically," Roxy said. Her voice sounded unnaturally loud like she was sitting right next to me. The helmet incorporated a headset that fit snugly over my ears, and her voice was coming to me through a Bluetooth link.

I wore jeans and a Patagonia jacket, which was the best I could come up with for a motorcycle ride. Roxy had grudgingly accepted that this outfit would do.

The pillion seat looked very high and exceedingly small.

"Am I going to fit on this?" I asked.

"They design these motorbikes for people who are very friendly," said Roxy. Her visor was still up, and I could see her smiling.

I am tall, so I was able to swing my leg over the bike. I sat down and got my feet on the pegs. They were *just* wide enough for the arches of my dress shoes. Roxy touched the electric starter, and I heard the characteristic growl of the powerful Ducati engine.

"It's definitely not Japanese," I said.

"Don't shout, Mr. Hancock," she replied. I had forgotten the Bluetooth and thought I was shouting over the noise of the engine. "No, it's not a sewing machine. You ready?"

"As ready as I'll ever be."

She snapped her dark visor down, and I did the same with mine. I braced myself with my hands on her shoulders.

"I'll blow you right of the back unless you hold me, Mr. Hancock. Put your arms around my waist and hang on tight."

"I'm not sure—"

"For the love of God, Mr. Hancock," she exploded. "We've just had sex. You can hold me tight."

I put my arms around her waist. It made me lean forward and brought my crotch up tight against the small of her back.

"I'm a small girl, Mr. Hancock. You'll have to hold me higher, just under my tits. That'll get you into the right position."

I did as she instructed. I felt the underswells of her breasts on my hands, through her heavy motorcycle jacket. *No wonder there is so much sexual innuendo around motorbikes*, I thought.

She opened the throttle, and the Ducati growled like a caged beast. She had her messenger bag on the fuel tank between her thighs, the strap still over her shoulder. She pulled out her phone and cued up a track with a heavy bass beat. Then she guided the bike around the narrow lanes of the underground car park and up the ramp into the street. I was pleased to see that the rain had stopped. However, the streets were still very wet.

As soon as she turned into traffic, Roxy opened the throttle, the Ducati roared, and I felt the rush as she ran through the gears. I could see the speedometer and rev counter over her shoulder, and we rapidly were at forty miles an hour in the narrow Mayfair lane. She cut around a delivery van and emerged into Piccadilly.

"Lean with me, Mr. Hancock," she said, her voice remarkably calm.

She sounded like she was sitting on a couch. Leaning the bike down to a deep bank, she moved her buttocks and thighs to a racing pose to maintain balance. I leaned, feeling as though my head was only inches from the pavement. She straightened and opened the throttle further. As we roared down Piccadilly, I saw the speedometer needle nudge sixty miles an hour.

"Roxy," I said, but the rest of what I was going to say died in my throat. We approached the Hyde Park Corner underpass, and both lanes were at a dead standstill. I braced myself for Roxy to hit the brakes, but instead, she accelerated and moved into the opposing lane. We were headed directly at a red double-decker bus. I closed my eyes.

Roxy trimmed the bike's direction, moving onto the double yellow lines. There were cat's eye reflectors on the lane markers, and our tires made a steady thumping sound as we ran over them. Roxy roared between the bus and a stopped truck, not slowing down at all.

She was all concentration, and her tension radiated from her taut body through my arms to me. We emerged out of the underpass and around the broken down car that had caused the jam. I breathed a sigh of relief as we got back into our lane.

As soon as we were in the clear, Roxy increased speed even further. The needle edged toward seventy. We just caught the lights at

Knightsbridge, zoomed past Harrod's, and turned on to the Curzon Road. The V&A passed by our right. Roxy weaved in and out of traffic, managing to catch green after green. There was so much action packed into the ride that it seemed like a long time had passed, but in reality, we were less than fifteen minutes out of the car park.

I braced myself as we banked around the Chiswick roundabout and got on to the motorway. Roxy gave the bike its head. The engine note got higher as the speedometer needle crept steadily upward. Eighty, ninety, and we were whipping past slower traffic. Roxy was literally dancing on the bike, squeezing between cars, getting on the shoulders of the motorway when necessary, but never allowing anything to slow her down. The needle was just over a hundred miles an hour now, and I gave up worrying. If anything went wrong now, we would be dead instantly. There would be no chance of survival.

The music was still pounding in my ears, and it blended in with the roar of the engine to create a feeling of invincibility. We were just approaching the Heston services when she took a hand off the handlebars and caressed my hands.

"Roxy, this is insane. We're going nearly a hundred miles an hour."

"I want to feel your hands, Mr. Hancock. We're nearly at the airport."

"Please put both your hands on handlebars," I said.

"Okay, if it makes you feel better," she said, complying.

"You're crazy, Roxy," I said.

"It's the closeness of death that sharpens the joy of life," she said. "I'd rather blaze for a brief moment like a shooting star than burn steady and boring like a candle."

"I'm steady and boring, Roxy."

"Not when you're feeling my tits at a hundred miles an hour."

I couldn't see her face, but it sounded like she was smiling. *I'm crazy too*, I thought.

The scenery and traffic continued to flash by for a few more minutes. Then all of a sudden, we roared into the Heathrow underpass, and a moment later, Roxy screeched to a halt front of the terminal where we thought Dolores would be. I was thrown against her back, mashing us even tighter against each other.

I put one foot down on the ground and tried to swing the other one over. My brain had not yet returned to stasis from our furious pace, and I was unsteady on my feet for a moment. Roxy put out a hand and steadied me.

"Go to your wife," she said. "I'll be waiting for you. Call me if you decide to fly back with her."

My helmet had unsnapped itself, and I pulled it off and handed it to Roxy. She took it with one hand and patted the front of my pants.

"Calm down, you crazy man," she said.

* * *

9

I looked back over my shoulder several times as I walked to the departures building. Roxy's visor was up, and she was engrossed with her phone. She did not look toward me, and I was curiously disappointed.

Once I was in the terminal building, I ran to airline counters, looking frantically for Dolores. She was tall and distinctive, and I saw her almost immediately, talking to an agent at the first-class counter.

"Thank you," she was saying. "Yes, that seat will be fine. Please make sure that my bags are transferred from the inbound flight back to this outbound one."

"Certainly, madam," said the agent.

"Doll," I said. "Can we talk?"

She turned around, clearly very surprised to see me. But she recovered quickly, and her face hardened.

"I told you I've had it with you," she said rather too loudly. "Just leave me alone, Jim."

"Please, Doll, I beg you," I said in a low voice. I was conscious that several people had begun to give us curious stares. "Let us find a quiet place to talk. Let me explain and try to make it up to you."

"Your actions speak much louder than words, Jim," said Dolores, her voice rising. "In bed with a prostitute as soon as you arrive in London. Disgusting man!"

Her raised voice quickly drew a small crowd, and a pair of the heavily armed anti-terror policemen sidled over to the fringes of it. I could see one of them thumb the safety off his automatic weapon.

"Please, Doll," I said, keeping my voice very low. "Don't make a scene. Let's discuss this in private like civilized people."

"Civilized!" she screamed. "You! I just found you in bed with an underage prostitute!"

"Don't say things like that, Doll." I still kept my voice very low, hoping it would calm her down, but it was a vain hope. I now had a fresh worry, for a regular policeman had joined the two anti-terror men. His ears pricked up when he heard Dolores scream "underage prostitute", and he began to move forward slowly through the thickening crowd.

"You've never achieved anything, Jim!" Dolores's voice remained loud, and the gathering crowd of curious bystanders was getting bigger. "You've been a drone your whole life just going into that office getting seniority like the furniture! Logan told me that all you've ever done is mark time. You've nothing to show for all your years at the bank! Nothing!"

"I supported you and the kids, Doll. We have a good life."

"You are never home! The children don't even know you. They hate you! Just spend all your time at the office—useless paper pushing! You're a poor excuse for a man! Who needs to pay a child to have sex with him!"

"Doll, don't say that." I said brokenly.

The regular policeman now pushed his way through the crowd and approached Dolores. He had another man in plain clothes with him.

"Excuse me, madam," said the man in plain clothes. "I am Detective Inspector Colton." He flashed a badge. "Are you accusing this man of having sex with a minor?"

Dolores hesitated for only a moment.

"Yes," she said firmly. "I was an eyewitness to this disgusting spectacle."

"Are you willing to make a statement?"

"Yes. Yes, I am."

The uniformed policeman now took my arm in his.

"We'd like to ask you a few questions, sir," he said. "Would you like to accompany us, please?"

"Doll, you know she wasn't underage!" I cried, no longer keeping my voice down as I was overwhelmed by fear and shame. I felt wetness, and when I touched my face, I realized that tears were running down my cheeks. "Tell these gentlemen! Please!"

But Dolores simply stood there with her hands on her hips. The uniformed officer's grip on my arm was not tight, but it was quite firm.

Then Roxy stepped out of the crowd. She was dressed in her motorcycle clothing with her messenger bag over her shoulder. She came up to plain clothes detective and stopped him with a hand on his arm.

"Inspector, I'm the woman this man had sex with this morning. I'm of age. Here's proof, my motorbike license."

She handed him a card. Colton, the plain clothes inspector, looked from the license to Roxy and then at Dolores.

"Is this the woman you saw this morning, madam?"

"Yes," said Dolores reluctantly. "Yes, she is."

"Well, she's not a minor," said Colton. He turned back to Roxy. "Did you perform sexual acts for money?"

"Mr. Hancock and I had sex," said Roxy. "But you'll never be able to prove that there was money involved."

I could see Colton's interest waning. It was unlikely that he was a vice cop, so this was probably not his interest anyway.

"Very well, madam," he said to Dolores. "Since you've identified this woman and she's not a minor, my colleague and I will be on our way."

The uniformed policeman released me, and the two of them walked away, pushing their way through the crowd.

"Doll," I said. "I'll go to counseling. I'll do whatever you want."

But she would not meet my eyes.

"Just go away, Jim. I can't stand the sight of you. When I tell them, the children will want you out of their lives as well."

My shoulders sagged. I felt a sob forcing its way up, tried to stop it but only succeeded in muting it. Dolores picked up her boarding pass from the agent and walked away toward security. The crowd slowly began to disperse. I watched Dolores disappear and felt my legs go weak. I was afraid that they would not hold me up and staggered over to a bench and sat down. I put my head in my hands.

I spent a lifetime building a relationship and a family, I thought, but I totally failed. My wife hates me. My children hate me. I'm a gray, boring, shell of a man, all alone with my data and quarterly results. I was crying again.

*   *   *

10

I did not know how much time passed. I felt completely drained as though I had just run a marathon. Slowly the scene around me coalesced. The busy airport crowds were going about their business. No one was paying any attention to me. My tears had dried on my face, but the salt tracks remained, powdery to the touch.

It took me several moments to become conscious that I was not alone on the bench. Roxy sat beside me, her hands daintily together on the lap of her leather skirt.

"Roxy," I said. "What are you doing here?" Then I remembered her role in getting me out of the clutches of the police. "Thanks so much for showing up and getting the police to release me. How did you know to come in?"

"People were streaming in to watch the scene, and I gathered from the chatter that it was you and your wife." She paused and put a hand on my thigh. "It was just evil, the way she tried to get you arrested. No matter what you'd done, there was no call for that."

"She's a high school teacher. She knows what fifteen-year-olds look like. She was probably convinced that you are underage. You do look young."

"Well, even if I was, she didn't care about me. She was trying to hurt you."

"Can you blame her? I've hurt her so deeply."

"Bah!" said Roxy derisively.

"I beg your pardon?" I said.

"She doesn't care two figs for you, Mr. Hancock. She only stayed with you because you gave her a lifestyle she could never have afforded on her teacher's salary. As soon as she saw a way to get your money without having to live with you, she grabbed it. I could see the dollar signs in her eyes when she said she was going to take all your assets."

"Roxy, you don't know her. We've been happily married for over twenty-five years."

"Really? All your assets are in her name. That doesn't sound like something a happily married woman would do. When was the last time she said anything nice to you?"

"Just a couple of weeks ago," I said immediately. "She told me how much her colleagues enjoyed the chocolates I got her from Zurich."

"How nice of her. You got her chocolates all the way from Switzerland, and she gave them away. When was the last time you had sex with her?"

"It was quite a while ago," I said weakly. "But it's not her fault. Dolores isn't tactile."

"Bollocks!" said Roxy.

"What?"

"I saw the way she looked at me when I walked toward her, naked. The look in her eyes was pure lust. She wouldn't let me past her. She blocked my way so she could stare at me. But I think she's too inhibited to seek out a lesbian relationship. She's sexually frustrated, doesn't understand why, and blames you. I think that's why she hates you. It's not rational, but I'd bet you ten quid its true."

"Dr. Roxy Reid, psychoanalyst," I said with a wan smile. "You're young and gorgeous. It's natural that anyone would stare at you, man or woman."

"Thank you, Mr. Hancock." She stood up. "Well, there's nothing more we can do here. But we have to leave now to make the meeting at four."

"I'd completely forgotten about that," I said. "I don't feel like going, but it would be awkward to miss it. Can we swing by the hotel? I need to change into a suit."

"Sure thing, Mr. Hancock."

She took a small lady's kerchief out of her messenger bag, wet it with her tongue, and wiped the salt tracks of my tears off my cheeks.

"You're a good man, Mr. Hancock," she said as we walked toward her Ducati. "She couldn't have made you cry if you weren't."

"Please don't tell anyone about the scene we just had at the airport," I said.

"I'm not a fool, Mr. Hancock."

She put her arm around my waist companionably. After a moment, I reached down and put my arm around hers.

*   *   *

11

I was probably getting used to Roxy's wild riding, so the trip back to London was less frightening. But every few moments, I still felt like I was going to die.

"I know nothing about you, Roxy," I said to her, hoping to slow her down with conversation. "Do you have any siblings? Where do your parents live?"

Roxy did not reply but gunned the throttle, causing the bike to surge forward so that I had to hold her even tighter.

"It's okay if you don't want to talk about it," I said hastily.

"No, it's not that," she said. "It's just that you would have a hard time understanding how I grew up."

"Try me," I said.

"Me mum was a crackhead," she said, her language and accent degenerating to her east London roots as she talked about her past. "She was a pretty little blonde thing, and she'd turn tricks with anyone who'd pay for her next high. So when she got pregnant with me, she had no idea who me dad is or was. She tried to have an abortion, but the back-alley quack that she went to botched it, and I lived, unfortunately for her. She never wanted me. She tried to put me into foster care as soon as I was born, but they wouldn't take me because they considered her a fit mum. God help us."

"That's just awful," I said.

She downshifted as we rapidly came up on the backside of a bus. The engine note rose sharply, and she slingshotted onto the shoulder to get around it. I was getting into the flow of riding with her now and felt the rush of adrenaline as we emerged from the close encounter with the large vehicle.

"You've probably seen stories about women like me mum in the papers. I was a huge encumbrance, so she often beat me, and her boyfriends beat me much worse. Even broke me bones a few times. Years later, I got the hospital reports. When I was seven, one of her boyfriends tried to rape me. I managed to wriggle free and ran out into the street in me underwear. That's when I literally ran into Nick Dredd. I was shivering, for it was December, and I had almost no clothes on. I don't know why, but he took an instant liking to me. He started visiting, and we got very friendly, nothing physical, just big brother-little sister stuff. None of me mum's boyfriends dared mess with me after that. Me mum died of an OD a year later when I was eight. I had no one in the world, but Nick showed up at the custody hearing and volunteered to take me."

"A known gang leader and a drug dealer," I said.

"Yes, but he pays off a lot of the people in the system," said Roxy. "He has to, otherwise, they'd shut him down and lock him up before you could say Jack Robinson. Plus, the foster care system is so overloaded that they are happy when anyone volunteers to take a child. Nick was good to me. He made me go to school and was really proud of me report cards. More proud than any dad would have been. And he was ever so pleased when I got me bike messenger job at fourteen and started racing bicycles. I moved out of his house as soon as I started getting paid."

"Why? If he was so good to you?"

"I knew where his money comes from, Mr. Hancock. Ever since I can remember, I've been trying to escape from the world me mum lived in."

"So you lived by yourself since you were fourteen?"

"Yes," she said. "I was quite safe, for everyone in the neighborhood knew that Nick was looking out for me."

"When did he become your boyfriend?"

"Oh, much, much later," Roxy said vaguely. "Nick isn't a pedophile."

I was surprised to see that we had arrived at the hotel. Roxy waited down in the lobby with her bike in temporary valet parking out front. I ran up and quickly changed into my suit.

* * *

12

My tie flew in the wind on Roxy's motorbike on the way to the office. She drove into the underground car park there, and we took the elevator up to the Eurobond department. I went with Roxy to her cubicle where she dropped off her motorcycle jacket and changed from her boots to a pair of chic stiletto heeled slippers with stylish ankle straps. She ran her fingers through her hair and said, "How do I look?"

While her leather skirt did not look out of place in the office, her sleeveless silk blouse was perhaps a bit too tight, and her steel-studded leather choker, nose ring, earlobe rings, and belly button ring were unusual to say the least.

"Unconventional," I said.

"I'll take that as a compliment," she replied as she headed for the meeting room, heels clicking.

I followed her. The meeting was in a corner room with a great view of the London skyline and the Thames. Julia was at the head of the conference table, and her analysts were seated already. There was a presentation already cued up on the screen.

"Mr. Hancock, welcome," Julia said. "Please take this seat." She pointed to the place at her right. She turned to Roxy. "Where have you been all day? There are a dozen things I wanted you to do."

They were a study in disparities. Julia was in her Chanel suit in banker's black, her short jacket over the archetypal white chiffon blouse, her distinctive snake choker necklace at her throat, and black stockings. She also wore high heels, so she was much taller than Roxy. Julia's mane of dark-brown hair was gathered in a professional bun at her neck and made Roxy's purple streaks seem even more out of place. Her brown eyes were a contrast to Roxy's baby blues.

"I was helping Mr. Hancock," said Roxy. "He asked for the pre-reading for this meeting."

"It took you all these hours to drop off some files?" Julia's tone was sarcastic. "You could have emailed them."

"I asked her to run some errands for me," I interjected before Roxy could reply. "She's been very helpful."

"Oh, that's all right then," said Julia, her face relaxing into a smile. "Well, now that you're here, make yourself useful, Roxy. Get me a latte."

Roxy left the room without replying. One of Julia's analysts, a big bear of man named Derek, began the presentation, going over the same documents that Roxy had already gone over with me. He was in his late twenties, good-looking in florid kind of way with straw-colored hair and gray eyes. He spoke with an upper-class Oxbridge accent. I could see why Roxy might have found him attractive. However, her story made me look at him with a jaundiced eye.

I was now giving him my full attention, but the presentation was too descriptive with very little analysis. Roxy's summary had been far more succinct. I raised my hand and made critical comments and suggestions at the appropriate junctures. Julia's analysts made notes of each one. I was surprised to find that even in his detailed presentation, I could not find anything over the gist that I recalled from Roxy. My opinion of Derek went even lower.

Roxy returned halfway through the presentation with Julia's latte and handed it to her. There was no seat for her in the room, Julia waved her away whispering, "I'll text you if I need anything."

But I stood up and interrupted Derek, saying, "I think Roxy should stay and listen. She can have my seat. I'm happy to stand."

"Are you sure, Mr. Hancock?" asked Julia, surprised. "She won't understand anything, but she can stay if you want."

Her staff brought in another chair, and Roxy squeezed in between Julia and me. She sat down and pressed my thigh with her hand, out of sight under the table. When I glanced at her, she gave me a look of gratitude that drove much of my despondency out of my thoughts.

The presentation, questions, and discussion went on for an hour. At five, Julia summarized my suggestions, and her staff made a list of action items for the Eurobond trading strategy over the coming quarter. They filed out, and I followed Julia to the corner office of the chief of the Eurobond desk. She'd moved in, and her photographs and mementoes were all set in place tastefully.

She shut the door and gave me a hug. This time, she pressed her body against mine like she used to.

"Thank you so much, Mr. Hancock," she said. She gestured at the view out of her floor to ceiling picture windows. London was at her feet. "This is all because of you. How can I ever repay you?"

"You've earned it, Julia," I said. However, Roxy's cynical estimation of Julia had injected a sour note into my feelings for her. I sat in one of the chairs by a window and looked out at the Thames. "So I hear you've been going out with Logan every time he comes through London?"

"Who told you that?" she asked sharply.

"Just rumors," I said.

"Of course, I have meetings with Logan whenever he is in town," she said, smiling. "But always at the office. You know how people gossip. With Logan's reputation, people assume that any girl that works with him is sleeping with him."

She sat down on my lap and put her arms around my neck. She leaned forward, and her soft firm breasts were in my face. With my nose between the buttons of her chiffon blouse, I felt the rough lace and smooth silk of her bra.

"It is so good to have you here in London, Mr. Hancock," she whispered. "I'm sorry I was so cold to you this morning, but I didn't want you to get the idea that we would be sleeping together. You and I know our relationship is delicate and ethereal, not physical. I've been thinking about you all day. You must be awfully lonely in your hotel, thinking about me."

She moved her bottom on my lap for emphasis. I put my hands on her narrow waist but did not feel the overpowering desire that she could normally elicit from me.

"We'll spend time together, like we used to," she whispered. "Platonic friends."

Instead of responding to her, I said, "Are you sleeping with Logan?"

She pushed herself away from me and put her hands on my chest.

"Mr. Hancock! How can you say that! Logan is even older than you. And I'm a happily married woman. Gunter gives me all that I can handle in the bedroom."

But von Hakenberg isn't making enough money to support his expensive tastes, I thought. *You need to increase your income, and sleeping with Logan would certainly help to do that.*

She stood up, smoothed her skirt, and walked over behind her large desk. I had a vision of Julia and Logan being intimate on it. Then her voice broke into my reverie and caused the vision to dissolve. I saw Julia sitting cool and composed in her high-backed swivel chair behind her desk.

"Shall I arrange for transport to get you back to your hotel?" she asked.

"No, I'll ask Roxy," I said.

"That's all right, then. I'll see you on Monday. Do you have plans for the weekend?"

"Not yet," I said.

She did not offer to meet me over the weekend. As I left her office and walked to Roxy's cubicle, I wondered what her plans were.

* * *

13

"I asked Julia if she is sleeping with Logan," I said to Roxy as she drove me back to my hotel on her Ducati. My voice sounded tinny through the Bluetooth link. "She immediately turned off the charm on me."

"She's sleeping with Logan," said Roxy. "I wasn't sure before, but this is confirmation. She wouldn't go cold on you unless she was sure that she had Logan's support. And Logan is a ruthless bloke, not a romantic like you. He wouldn't give her something for nothing."

My world seemed to be disintegrating around me. In the morning, I had been so sure that Dolores was my most loyal constant support and that my feelings for Julia were as pure as her character was worthy. Just hours later, both those bedrock beliefs were crumbling.

"I never thought of Julia as being so manipulative," I said.

Roxy laughed.

"That's an understatement," she said.

"You're probably manipulating me too, Roxy."

"I'm WYSIWYG, Mr. Hancock."

"WYSIWYG?"

"What you see is what you get. No subterfuge. I'm having sex with you, not pretending to love you."

"No one loves me," I said, feeling depression begin to envelope me again.

"Best not to think about it," said Roxy cheerfully. "You can take me out to dinner tonight. Later, I'll take you clubbing, if you're up for it. After all, it's Friday night."

I didn't want to be alone, so I said, "I'd like that."

* * *

14

I took Roxy to dinner at Langan's. It was a short walk from the hotel in Mayfair, upscale, but intimate, and not so stuffy that her attire and appearance would cause problems. The maître d' knew me, but he was too sophisticated to raise an eyebrow at my companion. I thought of making a joke about Roxy being my daughter's friend but decided against lying and let him think what he wanted.

I ordered a rather overpriced Chateau Margaux to go with our steaks. I was gratified to see Roxy dropping her hardened tough girl exterior and acting like an awed teenager for whom all this was very novel.

"This wine is excellent, Mr. Hancock!" she exclaimed with youthful enthusiasm. "I thought you needed experience to enjoy an expensive wine."

"You seem to have a sophisticated palate, Roxy," I said.

"Don't pull my leg," she said, laughing. "There's nothing sophisticated about me!"

We took our time over dinner, and it was past nine by the time I settled the check. We stepped out into a misting drizzle, so light that it barely got one damp.

"Let's go to Forty-forty in West Kensington," she said as we got back to her Ducati. "It's near where I live. Time Out said it's the hottest club in London right now."

"Okay, but only if you let me pay," I said.

We got to Forty-forty before ten. I was glad that I had had the good sense to sleep on the flight over and for my nap in the morning. The club was at the end of a narrow, rather dark alley. There was a long queue, but Roxy went up to the burly bouncers at the head and said something to one of them in a low voice. He nodded and opened the door for us. It was a step-down from street level and opened into a small foyer. There was a very attractive hostess by an inner door. She also smiled at Roxy and waved us in.

The club was darkened, and there was a jazz band playing on the stage. They were not too loud, but there was a good crowd on the dance floor. Roxy came up to the bar and greeted the barman, who leaned over and kissed her on the cheek. He cleared away two places for us, closing the tab of another couple, who vacated their barstools with noticeable reluctance.

"You seem to know everyone, Roxy," I said.

"I've come here once or twice, Mr. Hancock," she said dismissively. "I live around the corner."

We clinked glasses and sipped our drinks. Then Roxy handed her messenger bag and motorcycle jacket to the barman and led me to the dance floor as the band launched into an old favorite, "Stompin' at the Savoy." She was a very good jazz dancer, far better than me, but I tried to keep up with her. I'd signed up for dance lessons with Dolores when the children were little, but she soon tired of it. I had continued doggedly for some years, and those moves began to come back to me. Leading Roxy, I began to anticipate her moves and found myself dancing far better than I had ever done before.

"You dance well, Mr. Hancock," she said. "Have you had lessons?"

"Not for over twenty years," I said. "What about you? You're far better than me."

"Nick loves to dance," she replied. "He started me with lessons when I was little. He said the moves would complement my kickboxing."

"You do kickboxing?"

She nodded without answering. We took a break, and I went to the men's room. There was a queue, so it was a good fifteen minutes before I returned. Roxy was back at the bar, but there was a muscular young man with a swarthy complexion and thick dark hair on my barstool. He had his arm around her waist and as I came up, he pulled her to him and tried to kiss her.

"No!" said Roxy, struggling to push him away. "I said no!"

I walked up quickly and put my hand on the young man's shoulder, trying to pull him away from Roxy.

"She said no!" I said forcefully.

He released Roxy but balled his fist and hit me very hard in the face. I saw red and then black, and the next thing I knew, I was on the ground. He kicked my side and excruciating pain ran up my spine. I gagged, spluttered, and threw up my last drink, making a mess of my shirt front and jacket. He was going to kick me again when I saw Roxy slide off her barstool and prod him in the back. I don't know what she did, but he staggered a step before turning to deal with her. The crowd immediately parted, and there was clear circle of space around us.

"I'm going to fuck you, you white cunt!" he shouted.

Roxy moved so fast that I could not be sure that I saw what she did. She struck him in the solar plexus with a semi-bunched fist. It did not seem to hurt him much, but it caused him to bend over forward. She kicked him hard in the groin. Her motorcycle boot struck home with a loud splat. This hurt him a lot, for he screamed, put both his hands on his injured region, and doubled over. Now that she'd lowered him to her level, she kicked him again, this time striking his close-cropped head, her boot opening a big cut.

He fell heavily, and she straddled his chest. She began to systematically beat his face. There were sickening cracking and pulping sounds, but they did not seem to deter Roxy at all. Fortunately for him, the bouncers finally arrived, and two of them dragged her off him.

"Let me finish!" Roxy screamed. "I'll kill the motherfucker! Come on lads, let me go!"

"You're leaving, Roxy," said one of the bouncers, dragging her toward the steps leading out. "You can finish your business outside."

I followed the bouncers with Roxy. Other bouncers shouldered the muscular swarthy fellow and propelled him out the door. Roxy and I found ourselves out in the narrow dark alley with her victim. He sat with his back to the wall, blood running down his face. A moment later, one of his friends came out the door and pulled the battered fellow to his feet.

"She broke my bleeding nose, Mahmood," the fellow said, slurring.

"She broke a lot more than that, Yusuf," said his friend. "Come on, let's get you to the hospital. You're losing blood."

"Call the rozz, Mahmood," said Yusuf as his friend helped him out the alley. "The bitch is up for assault, she is. She's white. It's a racist attack."

We followed them out of the alley into the street, and the last thing I heard was Mahmood saying, "She's Nick Dredd's girl, Yusuf. The rozz won't touch her."

I was feeling quite dizzy and leaning a bit on Roxy.

"Who are the rozz?" I asked when we got to her motorbike.

"The police," she replied, straddling the machine. "Do you think you can balance? It's only a few minutes to my place."

"I'll manage," I said shakily.

* * *

15

Roxy lived in an end-of-terrace house on a rather nondescript street in west London. She had a small garage. It looked too narrow for a car, and she parked her Ducati in it. There were two Italian racing bicycles hanging from hooks in the ceiling and a variety of bicycle racing paraphernalia—cleated shoes, helmets, gloves, a floor pump—on the shelves.

The house was well-appointed with sleek modern Scandinavian-style furniture. As soon as we entered, Alfie, the Great Dane, galloped up, put his paws on Roxy's shoulders, and began to lick her face. Mercifully, he did not bark. It made for a picture of contrasts—the giant dog with his diminutive mistress. She petted and fussed over Alfie for a few minutes till he calmed down. He followed us into the small kitchen and lay down at Roxy's feet. She seated me at the tiny dinette, got an ice pack out of the fridge, and put it on my eye. She held it in place with a Velcro strip around my head.

"He landed a good one," she said. "You're going to have a right black eye."

I painfully took off my stained jacket and tie and hung them over the back of the chair. Roxy helped me take off my stained shirt and threw it by the washing machine. She gingerly felt my ribs one at a time. Then she opened a cupboard and took out a roll of medical strapping tape.

"It hurts when I breathe, Roxy," I said.

"He broke a couple of ribs when he kicked you, the wanker," she said. "I wish the bouncers had given me a few more minutes. I wanted to shove his teeth down his throat. He was lucky I didn't have time to get me brass knuckles."

She taped my injured ribs, saying, "Black eye, broken ribs—nothing a doctor can do. You just need time and aspirin."

"You really hurt him, Roxy," I said. The ice pack and the strapping tape made me feel much better. "You broke his nose and probably some facial bones as well."

I took both her hands in mine. She still wore her leather-Lycra fingerless gloves, and there was blood on them, though it was beginning to dry. I quietly pulled them off her hands. Her knuckles were raw with red, black, and blue bruising. I kissed them both.

"Thank you for saving me, Roxy," I said. "It was supposed to be the other way round."

She laughed.

"How many fights have you been in, Mr. Hancock?"

"I've never been in a fight, Roxy."

"So you've never hit anyone in your life?"

I shook my head.

"Ever been hit before?"

I shook my head again.

"And yet you stepped into a bar fight and took on this nasty bloke? To protect me? Did you think you could beat him?"

"I'm a man, Roxy. I had to try." I coughed. It caused severe pain in my broken ribs, and my face showed it. "I'm not a fool. I didn't think I could beat him. But I thought I could distract him long enough for you to get away."

"Did you seriously think I would run away and leave you to get the crap beaten out of you?"

"Sure," I said. "Like you said, you're just having sex with me, not pretending to love me. Our deal is simple. Sex in exchange for tutoring you and looking after you at work. Bar fights weren't part of the bargain."

She put her hands on both sides of my face tenderly.

"Silly boy," she said, but her expression was affectionate, and it made me glow inside.

"Roxy."

"Yes?"

"I…like you," I said. "You don't have to have sex with me any-more. You'll still be my special girl. I'll tutor you and watch over you at the bank."

"But Mr. Hancock," she said softly. "I want to."

*　　*　　*

16

Roxy led me up the narrow stairs to her cramped bedroom. Alfie silently padded up behind us. Almost all the floor space was occupied by a king-size bed. A narrow walkway around it led to an attached bathroom, and one wall was given over to closet doors entirely covered with mirrors. There was a large mirror on the ceiling as well.

"Wow," I said. "Who's your interior decorator?"

"When you have a small room, you need mirrors to make it look bigger," said Roxy though she sounded a bit sheepish. "It was really Nick's idea. He likes to see what he's doing."

"I thought you'd broken up with Nick."

"I have. But I get lonely, so I don't mind that he comes over once in a while and holds me." She took off her motorcycle jacket and boots and slid open a closet door to put them away. "Does that bother you?"

Somehow the thought of Roxy, so alone in the world that she would accept a man into her bed just so someone would hold her brought a lump to my throat. A fragment of poetry from high school came to my mind and I quoted:

> And sometimes thro' the mirror blue
> The knights come riding two and two:
> She hath no loyal knight and true,
> The Lady of Shalott.

"That's beautiful," she whispered.

"Tennyson," I said.

I sat on the bed with Alfie at my feet as she lit two aromatic candles on the bedside table and put out the lights. The ice pack had grown warm, so I took it off and watched her spellbound as she repeated her slow and spicy unbuttoning of her sleeveless silk blouse.

She culminated with a delicate shrug, and the silk slid down her smooth arms to drop on the floor. Her yellow silk bra looked much racier in the dim light. Her nose ring, earlobe rings, belly-button ring, as well as the steel studs on her choker, all glittered. The purple streaks in her hair and her crimson lipstick shone.

"My god, Roxy," I said. "A couple days ago, I prepared our bedroom for Dolores like this."

"You really know how to make a girl feel top of the world, Mr. Hancock," she said.

"But I was going to say, it was nothing like this!" I searched for the right words. "Dolores wouldn't even let me touch her. Whereas here I am with you, and you're a goddess."

"I've been called a lot of things," she said. "But no one's ever called me a goddess before. Has anyone ever called you a knight?"

"No," I said.

"You're my knight in shining armor, Mr. Hancock."

It was a repetition what she had done earlier in the day, and then again, it wasn't. She was much more gentle, and the expression in her eyes was so much warmer. It seemed like she was enjoying being with me rather than doing a job.

Afterward, both Roxy and Alfie crept up on the bed till she was sandwiched between us. She put her arms around me, and I let out a gasp of pain.

"Oh, I forgot your broken ribs, Mr. Hancock," she whispered.

She adjusted her hold on me and kissed my colorful black eye. She smiled at me, and the expression in her eyes made my heart melt.

I've been in London less than twenty-four hours, I thought. *In that time, I've ended my quarter century long marriage to Dolores, I've discovered that my grand passion for Julia was based on an illusion, I've been in a bar brawl for the first time in my life, and I think I've fallen in love with this girl-child who's far, far too young for me.*

Lost waif and formidable warrior, unschooled illiterate and genius savant, artless guttersnipe and sophisticated lady, childlike innocent and wise sage with trusting immaturity and weary cynicism—Roxy was an impossible bundle of contradictions.

"I'm so much older than you, Roxy," I murmured. "But I'd only ever slept with one woman before I met you."

"It's not a numbers game, Mr. Hancock," she said. "You're only the second man I've had sex with. But Nick gave me more experiences than a hundred men."

I don't know why, but this made me even happier.

"Roxy," I said.

I wanted to tell her that I loved her, but then my logical banker's brain stopped me. The vast difference in our ages, the fact that I knew her for less than twenty-four hours, our positions at the bank, and many other objections arose, like debits in a ledger.

"Yes?" she asked.

"Nothing," I said lamely.

The pleasure of her young body tight against me was still intense. But jet lag finally caught up with me, and I felt myself sinking into the oblivion of sleep.

CHAPTER 2

BLISS

1

My first weekend in London was a hectic whirl with Roxy. She drove me to the Cotswolds on her motorbike on Saturday, delighting in roaring down the narrow country lanes at perilously high speeds, feeding her thirst for adrenaline. I resigned myself to this as the price for her company and held on to her, grimacing as the pressure in the turns sparked pain from my broken ribs. We spent the night at the Taylor Hotel, an inn that was highly rated in my online searches. It was at the end of a long unpaved lane. Roxy complained bitterly about the effect of the rough road surface on her soft racing tires but was mollified by the inn's rustic atmosphere and upscale interior. The landlord and his wife treated us with traditional British reserve, and it was impossible to tell whether they were censorious when we asked for one room. They did look curiously at my black eye that had now developed a rainbow of colors.

Roxy liked the real ale that they had on tap and had pint after pint as we chatted. Then our hosts served us a delicious rack of lamb with a particularly fine mint jelly. We went through a bottle of red wine with dinner. With her small frame, she was tipsy by the dessert but insisted on joining me in a couple of glasses of vintage port. I half carried her up to the room and was quite prepared to just put her to sleep.

However, she grew quite amorous as soon as I shut the door. I threw her jacket over a chair, picked her up, and carried her to the bed. Having her under my control was new experience for me, and it accentuated my excitement.

The bed was a large four-poster that looked over a hundred years old. The springs creaked and groaned as I lay her on it and crawled in after her. I am well over six feet tall and became aware yet again of how little she was. The pain in my broken ribs was acute, but my desire for her was stronger. A storm had blown up, but I was focused on Roxy's luscious body. The thunder and lightning only played in my subconscious. It thrilled me to hear her cry out my name with genuine passion.

Afterward, we lay in each other's arms. I was tired but content.

"Strewth, I'm pissed," she said sleepily. "I forgot to take me pill this morning. Hope you didn't get me—"

She left the sentence hanging and fell asleep.

Roxy woke in the morning with a heavy head. I made her a cup of tea from the service in the room. She sipped the tea, then rolled out of bed and examined herself in the mirror.

"Crikey, I look like hell," she said.

I came up behind her and ruffled her hair.

"You look lovely to me," I whispered in her ear, playfully nipping at her earlobe rings with my teeth. I picked her up and kissed her.

"I'm feeling a bit queasy, luv," she remonstrated, so I put her down. She went to the bathroom and came out looking a bit happier.

I expected the storm to cover the sounds of our raucous love-making. However, by the way our landlady sniffed disapprovingly when she served our breakfast, it was clear that she had heard us. I hoped she hadn't been listening at the keyhole. But when I mentioned it to Roxy, she just laughed.

"I hope she was listening at the keyhole!" she said. "Maybe she'll get some ideas."

On Sunday, I rented a motorboat and drove Roxy up the Thames to Henley. We found a peaceful nook to moor the boat, surrounded by dense privet bushes. She'd ordered a picnic lunch hamper from Harrod's, and we ate it under the shade of a spreading willow, sitting on a thick blanket. We lazed and cuddled in postprandial indolence. We made love again in the lap of nature and received our just desserts when it began to rain on us. It was a sudden and heavy shower, and we were soaked in seconds. The rainwater ran down her shoulders, over her small athletic breasts to hang briefly on her nipple rings before dripping on to my chest.

She was panting, but I knew that she was still a long way from climax. I strove mightily to hold back but failed.

"I'm sorry, Roxy, I'm so sorry," I said, knowing that I'd given her yet another disappointing sexual experience.

"Shhh," she said, putting a finger on my lips. "I enjoy seeing you excited. This is real life, not a porno film."

"How did you know that I watch—" I began.

"You're a normal man with normal urges," she said. "When your wife refuses to have sex with you for months on end, what else would you do? You're too much of a straitlaced banker to pay for a whore or go out for a lap dance."

We gathered our wet clothes and put them on in the boat. I drove the boat back to London and settled up at the rental office. I kissed her and held her tight, conscious of the envious stare of the boat rental agent. She offered to take me back to the Mayfair Hotel on her motorbike, but it was raining harder, and I wanted her driving as little as possible in the downpour. She promised to text me when she got home. I got a taxi to the hotel and went up to my suite to pack. I was relieved to receive a text while I was packing, assuring me that she was safe at home, and delighted to see that she ended it with a big red heart emoji. I checked out, and the desk clerk got me another taxi.

The bank had rented me a serviced luxury flat in Canary Wharf, very convenient to the office, quite spacious, airy, and light, with great views. The furniture and fittings were first-rate, but in the manner of serviced flats everywhere, it was rather sterile. The decorations were predictable, with vases and bric-a-brac reflecting the tastes of some anonymous buying agent. The bareness of the walls was relieved by a few prints—Paris in the springtime, a Constable scene of the British countryside, a few abstract pieces.

*   *   *

2

My black eye elicited a lot of curious stares at the office on the Monday. Julia asked me about it, and I laughed self-consciously.

"You didn't go out clubbing with Roxy, did you?" she asked perceptively.

"No, no," I lied. "I haven't seen her since Friday. I ran into a doorjamb in the flat as I was moving in."

"I'm sorry to hear that," said Julia, looking skeptical. "Would you like to see our GP?"

"No," I replied. I quoted Roxy. "All I need is time and aspirin."

The first few days setting up my new office in the visiting executive suite were hectic. I got to work early, usually around six. The suite incorporated a corner office, but it was the one that none of the local senior staff wanted. It had the worst view. It looked out on to the dreary expanse of northeast London, unrelieved by any substantial landmark.

I began work with my Asian counterparties as soon as I got in. I was so busy that even though I thought about Roxy constantly, I was unable to find the time to see her outside of the office. My intense work schedule killed my sex drive, and I realized that this was how I had lived for decades with Dolores. I worked so hard that I came home too tired to think of sex, knowing that there was none available in my marriage bed.

However, I did see Roxy regularly at work. She made a point of coming in even earlier than me. As soon as I got through my first call, and sometimes during it, she would tiptoe in and place her latest assignments on my desk. I would quickly grade them while I was talking, making a few margin comments. She would go back to her cubicle, make corrections, and come back a few minutes later to show me. She invariably understood even my most cryptic notes and amazed me with the speed with which she learned. The financial markets foundation certificate exams were held six times a year, and the next available sitting was just over a month away. I was confident that she would pass them. In fact, sometimes she solved such difficult problems that I thought she would get the gold medal awarded to the highest scorer in every sitting.

"That's brilliant!" I exclaimed when she showed me her working on pricing a particularly complex forward position. "That deal involves solving for the base using today's FX rate and then pricing the forward. How did you know to do that? You've never traded FX."

"It stands to reason," she said. "We know the FX rate today with certainty, but we don't know what it will be at the forward date. If we use the estimated FX at the forward date, we're just introducing noise into the equation."

I just shook my head.

"Roxy, you're a genius," I said. "Even seasoned traders often get that wrong. I've got to show this to Julia."

"No!" she cried, snatching back the deal worksheet. "Don't tell her I'm taking the financial markets exams. She'll do everything she can to stop me!"

"Oh, Roxy, you're being paranoid," I said. "Julia will be really happy to see how well you're doing. After all, she hired you. This will make her look good."

"Please don't tell her!" Roxy implored. "I know her! It won't turn out well for me. Let me pass the exams first, then she can't take the qualification away from me."

I had never seen Roxy frightened like this, and it unnerved me.

"Oh, all right," I said.

"Promise me, Mr. Hancock! Promise me that you won't tell her."

"Okay, I promise," I said.

"On your honor as a gentleman," she insisted.

"I promise on my honor as a gentleman," I said solemnly.

*   *   *

3

My staff from headquarters trickled in over the next ten days and occupied the other offices in my suite. Getting everything running smoothly continued to keep me very busy, and I worked twenty-hour days, sometimes getting barely two hours of sleep in my flat at Canary Wharf. At the end of my second week in London, I realized that I had not seen Roxy for a few days. At a small break between meetings and calls, I walked over to her cubicle on the other side of the floor. There was a mousy young brunette with big glasses working there, and she looked up when I stuck my head in.

"Can I help you, sir?" she asked.

"I'm looking for Roxy Reid," I said. "I thought this is her cubicle."

"Oh, I don't know her, sir," she said. "I just started yesterday, and they gave me this cubicle."

"Julia must have moved her," I muttered to myself, but the girl overheard me.

"I'm Julia Pierce's new admin assistant, sir," she said. "Is there anything I can do to help?"

"New assistant!" I said sharply. She looked anxious, so I went on. "Oh, don't worry, it's not about you."

I went straight to Julia's office. I saw through the glass that she had some of her staff with her, but I pushed the door and entered anyway.

"Oh, hello, Mr. Hancock," she said. I thought her tone sounded a bit too sweet, almost like she was gloating. But perhaps I was imagining it.

"Can we talk in private, please?" I asked.

"Sure, Mr. Hancock," she said, waving her staff out.

"Julia, where's Roxy?" I asked as soon as the door shut behind them.

"I fired her the other day." Julia spoke with such elaborate casualness, that I was sure it was rehearsed.

"Why? I thought you liked her work. You were so up on her when I first arrived."

"Yes, I was. She's a fixer. But she's got a violent past and too many links to organized crime. I finally decided that it was just too risky for the bank to have her on the payroll."

"But you knew that when you hired her. What changed?"

"Really, Mr. Hancock, why are you so interested in Roxy? Is there anything I should know?"

"No, no," I said. "I just wondered what caused you to change your mind."

"Well, if you must know, it was in response to a complaint from one of my analysts."

"What did she do?"

"Why don't I ask him to tell you?"

Julia went to her glass door and beckoned to one of her staffs standing outside. He came in and stood self-consciously, shifting his weight from one foot to the other.

"Derek, tell Mr. Hancock about your experience with Roxy," said Julia.

Derek hesitated but took a deep breath and spoke.

"I asked Roxy out to dinner about a month ago. We had a nice meal, and she came back to my flat with me." He paused and looked at Julia, but she smiled encouragingly at him, and he went on. "We had sex, and when we were chatting after, the talk went to the hookers she had provided as part of the entertainment during the Sumitomo deal. I spoke of them rather disparagingly, and she got very angry. She reached into her bag and produced a switchblade knife and brass knuckles. She threatened to cut me and beat me. Of course, I was having none of that, so I threw her out."

"You claim you had sex with her, do you?" I said grimly. "And that you threw her out?"

"Yes," he said, not noticing my tone. "The next day at the bank I told her that she had better behave and that we would not tolerate her East End ways here. However, a few days ago, I caught her reading confidential deal materials in her cubicle. She'd obviously stolen them from one of the traders' desks. I suspect she was trying to sell them to a competitor. I immediately came to Julia and told her the whole story."

"So you see, Mr. Hancock, I discovered that I had been very wrong about Roxy. She was a dangerous liability. Suppose she had cut Derek with her switchblade? He could have sued us for millions, especially since I knew Roxy's background. And stealing deal materials!"

"Derek, you may leave," I said.

He looked rebellious for a moment but then thought the better of it and left.

"Derek's lying," I said as soon as the door closed behind him. "He tried to rape Roxy, and she defended herself. I've heard her side of the story, and I believe her."

"Mr. Hancock! Derek went to Harrow and Cambridge. Roxy is an East End drug dealer's girl. You can't possibly take her word over his. I know we live in the times of #metoo, but this is ridiculous."

"These 'deal' materials that Derek talked about. Did you see them?"

"I did," she admitted. "Derek got a bit overexcited. They were not real. They were practice materials for the financial markets exams. But that's private work. She's not supposed to be studying during office hours."

"Show me one of your analysts or traders that did not study during office hours," I said, my voice tight with suppressed anger.

"Just because everyone does it, does not make it right," she said defensively. "Look, Mr. Hancock, I don't know why you are so concerned about Roxy Reid all of a sudden. Is she sleeping with you? That's what a girl like her would do to get ahead."

"You don't know her," I said.

"You're my boss. If you tell me to reinstate Roxy, I will. But I will require it from you in writing. If anything goes amiss with her in the future, I want it clear that it is your responsibility, not mine."

I saw immediately that Roxy would never get a fair shake working for Julia. *She's been right about Julia all along*, I thought. *And how wrong I was!*

"I won't ask you to reinstate her, Julia," I said. "You're the chief of the Eurobond desk, and I won't undermine you. But you know that she cannot appear for the financial markets exams unless she is employed by a member bank. You're killing her dream, Julia."

"I don't see how I am doing that," retorted Julia. "She's doesn't understand the first thing about finance."

I bit my tongue and left her office. *I'll find a way*, I thought as I made my way back to my office. *I'll find a way.*

*   *   *

4

I had a huge list of things to do that had accumulated in my online work log. Mildred, my matronly assistant came into my office as soon as I returned from Julia's office. She'd been with me for over ten years and was extremely efficient in a cold mechanical sort of way. I depended on her implicitly. But I was not pleased to see her now.

"Hold everything for a few hours," I said. "I'll be back later in the afternoon."

"Are you sure—"

I didn't wait for her to finish but walked quickly to the elevators. I got a taxi at the rank down the road and gave the driver Roxy's address in West London. I rang the bell and waited, but there was no response. I heard Alfie's heavy paws as he came to the door and sniffed from the other side. He did not bark, and after a few moments, I heard him trotting back into the house. I called her cell phone, but it went straight to voice mail. I listened to her recorded message, happy just to hear her voice, and left her message to call me as soon as she could. I texted her that I was at her house.

A minute later, my phone buzzed with an incoming text. It was from Roxy. There was no message, just a map location. I tapped it open and zoomed in. It was a pub in the East End, the Wheatsheaf. It took me almost fifteen minutes to get a taxi in her neighborhood, but I finally managed to snag a black cab that was dropping someone off. I showed the driver the map location, and he nodded. I got in the back and noticed that it had begun to drizzle again.

The trip across London was slower than I would have liked, but eventually we got there. I paid off the taxi, hurried into the pub, and looked around. There were variety of sports playing on flat-screen monitors all around the barroom, and there were several slot machines along one wall. The interior was at odds with the pub's drab surroundings. The taps, bar, and furniture gave the impression of a much more upscale locale. It was fairly crowded with the lunch trade. The clientele was relatively young and looked well-off.

Roxy was at the bar, talking to one of the barmaids. She saw me but did not acknowledge me. She kept up her conversation with the barmaid even as I approached and stood by her. The barmaid looked at me questioningly.

"Roxy," I said. "Hear me out."

"I told you not to tell Julia," she said, without turning to me. "You gave me your word."

"I didn't tell her," I said, feeling like a little boy. "It was Derek."

"The wanker," she said.

"Yes," I agreed.

"Why are you here, Mr. Hancock? Julia sacked me. You don't have to fight for me. I'm just trouble."

"Did you seriously think that I would run away and leave you to fend for yourself?"

"You're stealing my lines, Mr. Hancock," she said, finally cracking a smile. "Do you want a beer?"

"It's a bit early for me, Roxy," I said.

But before I could continue, there was a shout from the door.

"Roxy!"

It was a tall powerfully built man, with piercing gray-blue eyes, and an Elizabethan beard. He was very handsome, although the right side of his face was marred by a thin white scar that went from his hairline to his jaw. He strode across the barroom and put his big hands on Roxy's shoulders, grinning at her.

"How've you been, girl?" he asked.

"I've been better, Nick," she said. "But it's good to see you."

A good-looking auburn-haired girl had entered with Nick. She came up and took his arm possessively, pulling it off Roxy's shoulder. She was dressed in the height of East End chic—a very, very short cerise satin dress with spaghetti shoulder straps. It was thin and so tight that it covered her like spray paint. Her voluptuous body was flaunted rather than concealed. She had on black ankle boots and a black satin choker ribbon.

"Hello, Roxy," the girl said, making no attempt to conceal her hostility. She was chewing gum, blew out a bubble, and allowed it to pop. "Those toffs in the City threw you out, did they? I guess they finally got tired of your third-rate blowjobs."

"I'm pleased to see you too, Tilly," said Roxy sweetly. "Do you want me to drag you to the loo and shove your face down the bog again?"

"You wouldn't dare! I'm Nick's number one girl now. Tell her, Nick!"

Nick looked embarrassed, but before he could answer, his phone rang. He looked at the screen and said, "I've got to take this. I'll be right back." He walked away from us to a quiet corner of the pub and sat down at a table, talking in a low tone.

"Hannah's sister works as a receptionist at your bank," said Tilly. "And she told everyone that you'd been sacked for stealing. What you do there is your business, Roxy. But you've got some nerve coming back here. After all the trouble you've just caused Nick."

Roxy's face registered surprise.

"What's she talking about, Maggie?" she asked the barmaid.

"The word is that you beat up a bloke at Forty-forty a couple weeks ago," said Maggie. "He's in hospital, pretty banged up—fractured skull, broken nose, broken cheekbones. He's Hamid Khan's cousin, a Brummie in town for a visit. The Pakis are pissed. Hamid's boys cornered Danny and Harry a couple days ago and beat the shit out of them. Now they're both in hospital as well."

"And Nick's beside himself," snapped Tilly. "The Russians are moving in on him, expanding out of their territory in St. Kat's Dock. The last thing he needs now is a war with the Pakis."

"How're Danny and Harry?" asked Roxy, her face showing very real worry.

"Lots of stuff broken," said Maggie. "But they'll live. They'll be off their feet for quite a while though."

"It's over then? Two for one? I'll go and see the boys today."

"No, it's not over, Roxy," snapped Tilly. "Nick met with Hamid Khan yesterday, but he's asking for the Whitechapel road as his price for peace."

"He can't expect Nick to give him that!" cried Roxy. "It's the most valuable piece of his territory!"

"You know how the Pakis are, Roxy," put in Maggie. "You're just a girl. You beat up one of their lads, you've made them all look like faggots."

"Fucking wankers," muttered Roxy. "It's all about their women-hating 'honor code'. Not that our lads are much better."

Roxy abruptly stood up and walked toward the door. Nick put his hand over the mouthpiece of his phone and called after her, "Don't worry about Hamid Khan, babe! I'll work it out with him!"

Roxy turned her head, smiled at him, and waved back. But she did not reply or stop walking. I followed her outside. She headed to her Ducati. Its bright red metallic paint was like a beacon across the road. Standing by her motorbike, she pulled her phone out of her messenger bag and tapped a call. I could hear her end of the conversation.

"Hi, Saira," she said. "It's Roxy."

She listened for a few minutes before speaking, and when she did, it sounded like she was interrupting.

"Yes, I know I've started a war. Look, no one's going to gain from this but the Russians. I'd like to talk. Can you meet me now?"

She listened for just a moment before saying, "Sure, I'll see you there. I'm on my way."

She tapped the motorbike's bar to unlock it and lifted her helmet off the fore bracket. I reached around her and unsnapped the second helmet from the rear bracket. She looked at me in surprise as though she was seeing me for the first time.

"What do you think you're doing, Mr. Hancock?"

"I'm coming with you."

"No, you're not. We're in the middle of a gang war. I don't have time to take care of you. Go back to your office."

"I don't care, Roxy, I'm coming along. Don't worry about trying to save me. That's what caused all this in the first place."

She shrugged.

"Don't say I didn't warn you," she said.

I put my helmet on, and we rode through an endless succession of twisting alleys. Soon it seemed like we had left England altogether, for the signage became dominated by the Urdu script that was totally unintelligible to me. Roxy braked sharply in front of a dilapidated restaurant front. Everything on the shingle was in the Urdu script except for two words in English—*halal food*. It was wet and miserable outside, and there was no one in sight on the street. We locked our helmets to the motorbike and went in. The interior was dim and dingy with a few naked forty-watt bulbs illuminating plastic chairs and rough wooden tables without tablecloths.

There was only one person in the room, an attractive girl about Roxy's age, wearing a shalwar kameez with a colorful chiffon *dupatta* scarf draped over her head. It was obviously for decoration rather than coverage, for her dark hair with its streaks of red henna was fully visible. She was very pale for a Pakistani and could have passed for a native of Southern Europe. But she looked tan next to Roxy's exceedingly white skin.

"Hello, Saira," said Roxy, pulling a plastic chair and sitting down. "It's been a while. But I see you've managed to keep a key to this place."

"Never know when you might need it," Saira responded. She had a working-class east London accent as well, but it was subtly different from Roxy's. "I haven't seen you since you rubbed my face in the mud at the Hackney Town Street Festival."

"You were a sport about that," said Roxy, putting out her hand. "You didn't tell your brother."

"It was between you and me, not between Nick and my brother," Saira responded, taking Roxy's hand and holding it.

"Well, I'm sorry," said Roxy. "Do you remember what it was about?"

"Some boy I fancied that you thought I shouldn't," said Saira. She laughed but quickly stopped. "It won't be so easy to clean this one up, Roxy. Who's this old *gora* you've brought with you?"

"He's my friend, Mr. Hancock. The one that your cousin Yusuf beat up."

Saira appraised me with a quick look up and down.

"Skinny," she said as though I could not hear her. "Not much meat on him. Can he fight?"

"No," said Roxy. "Your cousin is a fucking bully, Saira."

Saira sighed.

"Yes, Yusuf has always been an asshole. Now my parents want me to marry him. That's why he was down from Birmingham."

"So can you talk to your brother? Ask him to call off this war? Nick had nothing to do with this. I haven't been his girl for a long time now. Hamid has no reason to go to war with Nick."

"It's not that simple, Roxy, you know that. You beat up my cousin. That could be patched up, but he's my future husband and Hamid's future brother-in-law. A little girl like you! Our family honor is besmirched. There has to be payback, revenge."

"Is it all about honor and revenge? I heard that your brother asked Nick for the Whitechapel Road. That sounds like he wants money."

"Oh, that was just talk. Hamid never expected Nick to go for that. What he really asked Nick for was you. Nick got up and left without another word."

"I'm not Nick's to give!" said Roxy angrily. "Call your brother. Tell him that if he wants revenge, he can have it out with me."

"If Hamid and his men came here now, they'd rape and kill you."

I listened to this exchange with growing horror. We were in London, but this conversation sounded like something out of a lawless war zone.

"Roxy!" I cried. "Do you trust this woman? Her brother wants to kill you!"

"I've known Roxy since I was four years old, Hancock," said Saira before Roxy could reply. "We're girlfriends first, Pakis and whites second."

"But you said that she beat you up—"

"Where did you find this old *gora*, Roxy? He seems thick." She turned to me. "Roxy was my best friend. That's why she rubbed my face in the mud. Don't you get it?"

I didn't get it, but I subsided into silence. I felt like I was in midst of some strange tribe whose customs I did not understand at all.

"He's not thick," said Roxy. "Mr. Hancock is a brilliant banker. And I still consider you my best friend, Saira. I'll never forget that I always came to you after me mum's boyfriends walloped me. And you always gave me cuddles and stole *gulab jamuns* for me from this place. To this day, the taste of *gulab jamuns* brings back memories of beatings."

Saira leaned forward impulsively and ran her fingers through Roxy's hair.

"Poor Roxy," she whispered. "You were so frightened. Your big blue eyes like saucers. I wanted to kill those men that beat you!"

Roxy responded by putting her hand on Saira's cheek. The two girls seemed to be mutely exchanging a whole plethora of shared memories, and I felt like I was intruding.

"I'll call Hamid if you want," Saira said finally. "I won't tell him where we are. Don't agree to anything stupid. He's very angry right now—mostly at Yusuf for being such a wally and getting thrashed by a girl. But he'll never admit that, and he'll take it out on you."

Roxy put her hand out and grasped Saira's forearm before she could call.

"I just thought of something, Saira," she said. "Maybe we can make this work for both of us. You don't want to marry this Yusuf, right? There must be some family alliance involved."

"Yes," agreed Saira. "Yusuf's father owns a lot of shops and has property in Birmingham."

"Isn't there someone else you'd rather marry? You've always had a lot of admirers."

Saira blushed prettily, a surprising transformation for a girl who had just being talking about raping and killing.

"I like Iftekhar Salim," she said, sounding coy. "He came for my cousin's *nikah*, and we talked all night. We still meet in secret. He picks me up in the afternoons, and we go to hotels in the West End."

"Have the two of you had sex?"

"Just once," said Saira.

"You always were a risk-taker, Saira. If your brother found out, he'd cut your throat."

"Yes, he probably would," said Saira agreed.

"Wait," I said, unable to contain myself. "He's your real brother? The same mother, the same father? And he'll kill you for sleeping with a man? Wouldn't your parents stop him?"

Saira gave me a contemptuous look, and then said to Roxy, "Are you sure he's not thick, Roxy? He sounds awfully stupid."

"He just doesn't know orthodox Pakis, Saira." She turned to me. "In some ways, Saira's family is very old-fashioned. If a girl loses her virginity before marriage, it's a stain on the honor of the family that can only be cleansed with her blood. If they found out, Saira's parents would *encourage* Hamid to kill her."

"It's tough bein' a girl," said Saira. "'Snot that easy for a white girl like you either."

"No, it's not," said Roxy. But then she returned to her original line of conversation. "The Salims are crazy rich, right?"

"Yes, have been for generations. Iftekhar's parents suspect we're seeing each other, but they've never met me. They know my family though. We're not good enough for them."

"It'd be quite a coup for your family—to get hitched to legitimate old money. Why don't we play it like this—you tell your

77

brother that you can't possibly marry a faggot like Yusuf. He couldn't even protect you from a girl, for Christ's sake. Tell him that you have a much grander alliance in mind, so Yusuf is no longer part of your family's inner circle. Hamid's already sent two of Nick's best men to hospital. That's revenge enough for a Brummie shopkeeper cousin."

"Iftekhar's parents will never accept me—" Saira began.

"Wait, I'm not finished. Mr. Hancock, do you know the Salims?"

"Yes," I said. "The bank holds a sizeable portion of their corporate debt. They're worth a lot of money. They own property all over the world."

"Can you meet with old man Salim and give him some crumbs? A few beeps on a corporate bond issue? Take Saira with you. You'll have to say that you're an old family friend of the Khans and that she happened to be visiting with you. It'll be a good start for him to see what a fine modest God-fearing girl Saira is. A few white lies will help too. You could say that her brother banks with you. And that he has significant financial assets at the bank. Money always talks to rich people."

"High net worth asset management is not my department," I said. "But I can probably finesse something. And it will be much better if Saira's brother actually opens an account with us. That will give me cover as well when I vouch for him."

"How much money are we talking?" asked Saira.

"At least a hundred thousand pounds," I said. "If that's too much—"

"Hamid has twice that much lying around in cash," said Saira. "But he doesn't trust bankers. He's been talked into investing in financial instruments before and lost money."

"Mr. Hancock can put together a totally safe package for him," said Roxy.

"Okay," said Saira dubiously. "I'll talk him into putting up a hundred K. He won't like it, but he'll do it if I tell him it's for me."

"Saira can twirl Hamid around her little finger," Roxy said to me. "He loves her to death."

"To death indeed," I said sardonically. "He'd kill her if he knew what she's done."

"He'd kill me because he loves me," said Saira. "It would break his heart, but he'd do it for the family."

"I'm sorry, Saira," I said. "But I'll never understand."

"How soon can you arrange a meeting with the Salims?" asked Roxy, once again steering the conversation back to what we were discussing.

"I'll have to go to my office and check," I said. "With the volume of business they do with us, I am sure I could find something to talk to them about in the next few days."

"Good," said Roxy. "Saira, try to stop your brother from doing anything crazy for a couple of days. I'll do the same with Nick. And I'll be in touch as soon as we have a meeting set up. I'm depending on you to prep Iftekhar so he can be there to push things forward. Do you have something suitable to wear?"

"Iftekhar loved me in the red and gold lamé sari I wore at my cousin's *nikah*." She blushed again. "He told me several times it made me look like a bride."

* * *

5

Roxy and I emerged from the meeting with Saira, put our helmets on, and straddled the motorbike.

"I'll drop you at your office," said Roxy.

"Why don't you come up with me?"

"Julia had me escorted out of the building by security when she sacked me. They took my access card and told me not to enter the building again."

"I can get that reversed, but it will take a day or two," I said.

"I need to see Danny and Harry at the hospital anyway," she said. "I've known Danny since I was little. I feel terrible about this."

I held on to her tightly as she cut through the lanes at high speed. Her fat rear Pirelli racing tire generated a rooster tail of spray behind me. My phone rang and I pulled it out of my jacket pocket, adjusting my hold on Roxy for a moment. She slowed to allow me take the call. I looked at the screen and saw that it was from Richard

'Bud' Brewster, my lawyer back home. I tapped the screen and was surprised to see it automatically sync with my helmet Bluetooth.

"Bud!" I said, trying to sound hearty. "What's up? It must be very early in the morning there."

I put the phone back in my jacket pocket, pleased with the hands-free Bluetooth connection. Roxy sped up again.

"Yes it is, Jim. I just got in." His voice came through the helmet speakers, much clearer than through the tiny speaker on the phone. "How're you doing over there across the pond?"

"I've been crazy busy setting up my office in London," I said. "Lots of staff to settle in, moving the entire global operation to London. I haven't had a spare moment."

"Well, I'm sorry to bother you at a time like this, Jim. But there was a detailed communication from your wife, Dolores, waiting for me this morning through her lawyers. She's retained the most prestigious attorneys in the city. She's suing you for divorce, Jim. And she wants everything—every last cent of yours. If half of what she alleges is true, we'll have a hard time stopping her."

In the first flush of guilt over cheating on Dolores, I had been quite willing for her to get everything. But now, after a few days' reflection, and particularly after my joyful times with Roxy, I was not so sure.

"I'm all ears," I said as we passed the Mile End tube station and approached Mile End Park.

"She alleges that she caught you having sex with a child prostitute in London. She has pictures. She says you had an affair with a young female houseguest you had a few years ago. All this is in addition to the usual claims of mental cruelty, neglect of family and children, etc., etc."

I felt tightness in my chest. I hadn't had an affair with Julia, at least not one that would be recognized by a court of law. But then I thought of all the bank staff that saw me canoodling with her in public. Everyone *thought* I was sleeping with her. My pride in my non-affair had come back to haunt me.

"What does she say about the affair?" I asked.

"She alleges that it was a woman who reported to you at work."

"Nothing else about the young houseguest? Does she name her?"

"My God, Jim, isn't all this bad enough?" Bud sounded quite shocked at my questions. "Is there more to tell? You better come clean with me. We don't want to be blindsided later in the process. And to answer your question, yes, she does name the houseguest. Julia Pierce, the daughter of an old friend of yours."

"Yes," I said. "That's her name. But I didn't—"

"Jim," said Bud, interrupting me. "I'm telling you right now, as your lawyer, that if this goes to trial, you're toast. You're going to look like the world's dirtiest old man. In the current atmosphere, this could cost you your job. In fact, if I was you, I'd be worried about Dolores sending a copy of this dossier to your bank president, Logan Baldwin. If all this became public, no other bank would touch you."

"I know, Bud," I said. "We've got to settle. We can't let this go to trial. What do you think you can salvage for me in a settlement?"

"Well, she'll definitely get the house, your place in the Hamptons, and your ski lodge in Vail. I think we should ask for half of your financial assets, your retirement account, your condominium in the city, and your Mercedes. We can claim that you need the condo as a roof over your head and that your car is essential transport. And we can bargain down from there. You've made things difficult for yourself by putting everything in her name. "

"What's a realistic end point, Bud?"

"I'm afraid we're in a very weak bargaining position, Jim. We'll probably end up giving her a lot of your current financial assets. I'm hoping that her lawyers will see that taking your assets up front will be easier to implement than garnishing your future incomes and going after your retirement accounts. I'll try very hard to save your condo and your car."

Thank God the bank is paying for all my expenses in London, I thought.

"I'm left with a one-bedroom condo, a car, and a minority share of my assets," I said. "That's a heavy price to pay. But I guess I've made my bed. I have to lie in it. I'll go along with whatever you advise, Bud."

There was a brief silence on the line.

"Jim, what were you thinking? What were you doing with a child prostitute for Christ's sake?"

"She's not a child, Bud," I said.

"I've got the pictures right here in front of me, Jim. She looks fifteen, a kid!"

"She's of age, Bud." I paused for a moment before going on. "I can't explain it. All I know is that I feel alive for the first time in my life."

"I've been your lawyer for a long time, Jim," said Bud. His voice sounded heavy. "I'm in your corner. I'll do all I can for you."

I saw the signs for the Whitechapel tube station. It had started to drizzle again.

*　*　*

6

Just five minutes after I ended the call with Bud, my phone rang again. I pulled it out of my pocket and looked at the screen. It was my daughter, Heather. She was always busy when I called, rarely responded to my texts and emails, and never acknowledged the gifts I often sent her. So this was a pleasant surprise. I tapped it open and put the phone back in my pocket again.

"Hello, baby," I said, using the epithet I always used with her. "It's so great to hear from you!"

"Hi, Dad," she said, her voice sounding ominously somber. "I'm embarrassed to call you that, but I guess the relationship is a fact of my life."

Dolores must have talked to her and painted me as black as she could.

"Do listen to my side of the story, baby," I said quickly. "It's not as simple as your mother probably made it sound."

"Are you're going to deny that you were fucking a child prostitute? Deny that you had an affair with Julia?"

"That's all twisted," I said. "Listen to me, Heather—"

"It just makes my flesh crawl. I used to have lunch with Julia every other day that summer she lived in our condo! All the while, you were sleeping with her! I'm sorry, there's nothing more to be said. I'm just calling to tell you that I don't want to see or hear from you ever again. I'm going to tell my fiancé, Rob, that you died. I wish you really were dead, at least then, mom would get your life insurance. I'm asking Uncle Charlie to walk me down the aisle at my wedding. Goodbye."

"Wait!" I cried. "You're getting married?"

But she had already cut the line.

I was desperate to learn more, so I pulled out my phone again and searched till I found my son's number. I tapped it and waited till it began ringing before putting the handset away again. It rang and rang, and when it was finally picked up, I heard Nathan saying, "Hello!"

"Hi, Nathan!" I began, infusing as much warmth into my voice as I could. But then I realized it was his voice mail.

"This is Nathan Hancock. I can't come to the phone right now, so please leave a message."

"Hi, Nathan," I repeated after the beep. "This is Dad. I just heard that Heather is getting married. Could you give me a call? I'd love to hear more about it."

I tapped the call closed and looked out through the raindrops on my helmet visor for a few moments. Hope gave way to resignation; it was very unlikely that Nathan would respond. I slowly came to terms with the reality of my situation. My son hadn't been in touch with me for over a year. My wife hated me. And my daughter wished me dead.

*　　*　　*

7

We got to the bank, and Roxy braked in her usual sharp manner, causing me to mash up against her. She did not allow the machine to come to a complete stop but allowed it to roll forward. She nosed around to the motorcycle parking stripes at the corner. She dismounted after me and clipped her helmet to the fore bracket as I clipped mine to the rear one.

"I thought you said you couldn't enter the building," I said.

"I feel a sudden urge for a coffee, Mr. Hancock. Would you like to join me?"

There was nothing I wanted to do more than spend time with Roxy, so I agreed with alacrity. We walked a short distance to a coffee shop in Coleman Street. It was fairly quiet. The lunch rush had subsided, and the midafternoon coffee hour was still some time off. I got a double espresso for Roxy and a macchiato for myself. We settled at a corner table with a nice view of the street.

"Do you think the Salims will accept your friend Saira?" I asked. "They're awfully rich and snobby, you know. Old man Salim is angling for a peerage. He won't be happy to be related to a drug dealer."

"It's a two-track strategy, Mr. Hancock. In this day and age, Iftekhar Salim has a say in it too. Saira can be a bewitching enchantress when she turns it on. I've seen her in action. When she plays with her *dupatta* or sari *pallu* and bats her long black eyelashes, she has the boys competing for her attention and handles them like puppets. This Iftekhar would have to be made of stone to resist her. The parents will make a fuss, but I don't think they will risk losing their son. The financial sops and façade of respectability you offer will swing the balance."

"You're quite the strategist, Roxy," I said, smiling. "Does Nick know that you're saving him from a gang war?"

"No, of course not!" she exclaimed. "He doesn't know about Saira and me. Neither does her brother, Hamid. None of them do. You've got to understand, we're from warring clans, Mr. Hancock. School used to be a neutral zone, and that's where we met. Out of school, we met in dark alleys, the crypts of old graveyards, and off hours in that restaurant of her uncle's. We spent hours together, just chatting about nothing. Her family adores her, but they smother her with rules. In a way, we're both street children."

"Nick is lucky to have you on his side, Roxy," I said.

"Nick saved my life. He made me who I am." Her espresso had gotten cold, but she sipped it anyway. "I heard you talking to your lawyer. And your daughter."

"How?" I asked, my shock showing on my face. "I was on a closed Bluetooth link."

"The two helmets are synced together," she said. "I'm sorry, I should have told you. But once you took the call from your lawyer, I didn't want to interrupt."

I flushed. She'd heard all the details that had brought on my daughter's disgust. My relationship with her—referring to her as a child prostitute—must have sounded sordid.

"I'm sorry you're getting dragged into my divorce," I said in a low voice. "You have every right to be angry. But I swear to you on my honor as a gentleman that I will not identify you in court, no matter what they do to me. And I did not sleep with Julia."

She put her hand on my wrist and squeezed it.

"You're an incredibly naive man, and Julia is a sensual manipulative woman. I can imagine what she did." She sipped her cold espresso. "I had a hard time keeping my mouth shut when your daughter was so mean to you. She's going to keep skiing at your lodge in Vail, isn't she? And summer in your house in the Hamptons. And be subsidized with the money you made pulling all those bleary all-nighters at the bank. Along with her mother and brother, she's going to steal everything you worked so hard for! And she wished you were dead! The father who gave her everything!"

I was astounded to see that her eyes were moist.

"If I had a dad like you, I would love him with every fiber of my body," she said, big tears forming in her eyes. She hastily wiped them away with the back of her hand. "Did you mean it when you said that with me you feel alive for the first time in your life?"

I put my arm around her shoulders and nuzzled her hair with my face.

"Yes, Roxy," I said.

She turned her head up and kissed me.

* * *

8

I told Roxy to keep studying for the financial markets exams, and she met me the next morning at 6 a.m. at the coffee shop in Coleman Street so I could grade her work. I quickly scanned it as I sipped my coffee, made margin notes, and gave her some readings that would help her understand my comments. After a lingering kiss that drew stares from the other patrons, I regretfully left her to go to work. The first thing I did was go to the Director of Human Resources to rehire Roxy to my personal staff.

I was shocked to find that I could not do so. In her termination letter, Julia had cited a 'breach of bank regulations' as the reason for sacking her. This meant that it was legally impossible for her to be offered another position in the bank unless Julia rescinded her letter. And I knew she would not do that.

However, I was not giving up so easily. I went back to my office, picked up the phone, and called Hunter Chadwick Bain III, the London principal of Bain Jennings, a New York white-shoe investment bank. He went by 'Chad', and I'd done a lot of work with him over the years.

"Hi, Chad," I said. "It's Jim."

"Jim! I heard you were over, setting up your operation here in London. What's up?"

"Actually, Chad, I have a small favor to ask," I said. "Though in time, I think you'll come to realize that it is me doing you a favor."

"Now you're making me nervous," he said, laughing.

"I have a young woman I'd like you to take on as a trading assistant. She'll take the next round of the financial markets exams."

"Ask her to come see me," said Chad, his tone neutral. "Where did she go to school?"

"I'll tell you what, Chad. I'll bring her over. Then you can see for yourself. When's a good time?"

"I have some time late this afternoon. Just after the market closes would be good."

"Fine. We'll be over then."

I sent Roxy a text to meet me at the coffee shop in Coleman Street at a quarter to five in the evening. I was gratified to receive a nearly instantaneous response, "Okay."

* * *

9

Roxy and I walked from the coffee shop to the Bain Jennings office. It was only a ten-minute walk, and we got there just as the markets were closing. Chad's secretary told me that he was expecting us and waved us in. His office was huge with heavy old-fashioned furniture as befitted a prestigious white-shoe establishment. There was a real fire in the grate and an expensive crystal decanter on a side table that I assumed contained a fine brandy.

He was on the phone with his eyes fixed on the two big trading terminals on his desk. I assumed he had the market close up there. He said, "Yes, yes, we'll do it your way," hung up, and beckoned us forward. He looked at Roxy with barely concealed surprise.

"Chad Bain, Roxy Reid," I said, making the brief introduction.

Chad came around his desk and shook Roxy's hand, then looked at me questioningly.

"I thought you were bringing over the girl you were recommending we take on as a trading assistant."

"Yes, this is her. Roxy can work through complex financial problems faster than anyone I know."

"Jim, you're one of the brightest people I've ever met in this business, so I'll take your word for it." He turned to Roxy. "What are your qualifications?"

"I'm sorry?" Roxy sounded puzzled.

"Where did you go to college? I guess you call it university over here. We normally only hire from Oxford and Cambridge."

"I haven't been to university, Mr. Bain."

"What are your A level results?"

"I don't have any A levels. I have six GCSEs though. I had the best scores and the most GCSEs of anyone in my school."

Chad literally took a half step backward.

"And where did you go to school?"

"Eastberry School in Barking. It's in east London."

Chad looked at me.

"Jim, is this some sort of joke?"

I realized that I had been too hasty. My enthusiasm for Roxy's abilities had blinded me to how she must appear to someone who did not know her.

"Chad, listen to me. Roxy has a razor-sharp mind. I've seen her work."

"A genius who has no A levels, from east London, who sounds like she should be serving drinks in a bar." I opened my mouth, but he put his hands up to forestall me. "I'll take her on, Jim, but only as a special favor to you."

"Let's go, Mr. Hancock," said Roxy, taking my hand. "I don't want charity."

I let Roxy pull me toward the door. Once there, I turned around.

"Chad, Roxy will make a believer of you, I promise."

"I'm all for equal opportunity and upward mobility, Jim. I'm an American like you. But if she wants to be hired on her merits, there has to be *some* documentary evidence of her ability."

*   *   *

10

We walked down the three flights of stairs to the street, and just as we were leaving the building, I got a brain wave.

"Chad wants documentary evidence," I said. "We'll give him documentary evidence. Come with me."

I pulled out my phone and tapped it to search for the address I wanted. I found the phone number and called.

"We have twenty minutes," I said, showing her the address on my phone. "Can you get us there?"

"Piece of cake," she said.

We walked to her Ducati, and she got us there in ten.

I led the way into an older office building and up a flight of worn wooden stairs. There was an office with a frosted glass door at the top with the words "Mensa, London" on it. I pushed it open. The was only one person there, a rotund bald man about my age.

"I'm James Hancock," I said. "I just called."

"Yes," he said. "Is the young lady ready to take the entry test?"

"Wait, what test am I taking?" asked Roxy suspiciously.

"It's the test to see if you can apply to Mensa," the rotund man said. "If you score above the cutoff, you can take the full test. Mr. Hancock is one of our international board members, and he's asked me to administer a special test for you as a favor to him."

"Why am I doing this, Mr. Hancock? Your friend already said that he wouldn't hire me, except as a charity case. He said I sounded like a barmaid. This test won't change that."

"Roxy, it's a chance. If you can get admitted to Mensa, it will certify what I said, that you're very, very bright. Chad said he wanted documentary evidence. This is documentary evidence."

"You heard him, Mr. Hancock. He said they only hire from Oxford or Cambridge."

"It's the only chance we've got, Roxy," I said. "You've got to take it."

"Oh, all right," she said with bad grace.

The rotund man produced a laptop and cued it up for the application test. It was a thirty-minute IQ test. He led Roxy into a featureless inner test room, sat her down, and returned to sit at his desk. He resumed reading something on his computer screen and did not appear to want conversation. I sat down on one of the visitor chairs and tapped my phone nervously, answering emails. There was a big clock on the wall, and I watched the minutes tick by. Twenty minutes later, Roxy emerged with the computer in her hands.

"You have another ten minutes," said the rotund man.

"I'm done," she said.

"Go back and check your work, Roxy," I said. "You have time."

"No, I'm done, Mr. Hancock."

The rotund man took the laptop and hit a few keys to produce the score. His expression did not change, but he said, "You've got a perfect score. You've qualified to take the formal test."

I let out a whoop.

"That's great, Roxy! I knew you could do it!"

"Does she want to take the actual test right now, Mr. Hancock?"

"Yes! Yes!" I cried.

"Must I?" asked Roxy. "It won't do any good, you know."

"Roxy, you've got to do this," I coaxed. "It will be a good thing to have no matter what happens."

The rotund man worked on the laptop for some time and said, "We're ready. There's a timer on the test that's synced into my computer here. As soon as you hit start, the timer will begin counting. You have one hour."

"A whole hour!" complained Roxy. "What a waste of time!"

But she took the laptop and disappeared into the test room again. We repeated the waiting game. About thirty minutes later, Roxy emerged again.

"Done already?" I asked, surprised.

"No, I got bored. I've done all that I want."

The rotund man took the laptop and said, "You've only done two-thirds of the test. Do you want to give up?"

"Roxy! Don't do this! Go back in and finish it. Please!"

We argued for another ten minutes before she finally said, "Oh, all right, Mr. Hancock. You're being a real pain about this."

She went back into the test room and reemerged ten minutes later. She handed the laptop to the rotund man without a word.

My heart sank, for it was obvious that she'd done the rest of the test in a slapdash lackadaisical manner.

The rotund man produced the score again and looked at Roxy, still without expression. "You scored 130 on the Stanford-Binet scale. You're two points below our cutoff. I'm sorry."

I realized it would be counterproductive to berate Roxy now.

"Can you give us a formal result report? And document how close she got to the cutoff?"

"The official score sheet will indicate that," the rotund man said. "It is printed as a matter of course. It will cost you fifteen pounds though."

I pulled out my wallet and counted out the money. He folded the score sheet and put it in an official Mensa envelope.

"Where to?" she asked when we got back to motorbike.

"Let's go back to Chad's office," I said. "We've nothing to lose."

She shrugged and put on her helmet but did not respond.

*   *   *

11

It was dark when we got back to Chad's office. There was a security man in the lobby, and he called Chad's office before unlocking the elevator for us. Chad's secretary was gone, and the lights everywhere were turned down. However, his office was still brightly lit, and he came out to lead us in. He took a seat behind his desk and motioned us to the chairs in front of it, looking at me questioningly.

"You asked for documentary evidence," I said, putting the Mensa envelope on his desk and sliding it forward.

Chad took the envelope, opened the flap, and pulled out the report. He studied it carefully for a few moments.

"One thirty," he said. "Top 2 percent of the population. That's pretty good." He slid another piece of paper toward me. "Here, take a look at this."

I picked it up. It was a difficult fixed income portfolio decision problem, based on a term structure of interest rates. I worked out the answer mentally and looked up.

"Give it to Roxy," said Chad.

"That's not fair, Chad. This isn't just problem solving. It involves strategic decision making as well. It requires market experience."

"That what we sell here, Jim. Strategy advice. We're more than a bond trading house."

"Roxy, work out the prices first," I began as I handed her the sheet.

"Just give it to me, Mr. Hancock," she said.

She examined it carefully, then pulled a pencil from her messenger bag. She quickly wrote on the sheet in a childish but neat block script. It took her about ten minutes to write three detailed notes. She passed the sheet back to Chad across his desk.

He took the sheet and read her notes in silence. His face was study, for he was clearly stunned. He went over her notes several times as though trying to convince himself of the reality of what he was reading. Finally, he looked up.

"These are very good," he said. "All three of these options are in the money."

"They seemed to be the only viable options," said Roxy.

I reached forward, picked up the sheet, and went over her notes. She was wrong—her options were not the only viable ones, and they were not as good as the optimal solution that I had worked out. But all three were technically correct and in the money.

"A girl with no 'A' levels," said Chad, shaking his head. He sounded like he was in a daze.

Then he got up, walked around his desk, and stuck out his hand.

"Ms. Roxy Reid, I'd like to offer you the position of trading assistant at Bain Jennings. I hope you will join us."

"I'm happy to accept," said Roxy, standing up and shaking Chad's hand.

"I'm sorry I doubted you, Jim," said Chad as he escorted us out. "But you must admit that Roxy is a bit—"

"Unconventional," I said, finishing his sentence.

*　*　*

12

I didn't see Roxy for the rest of the week. My work at the office consumed me, and I was back to sleeping barely four hours a night. I managed to fit in some very short runs to maintain some level of fitness, but my ribs prevented me from attaining any speed. I could not believe how much pain I was in from this relatively minor injury.

I found time to call Shaheed Khan Salim in the middle of the week. As Saira had said, the Salims were old money, and he spoke with a characteristic Oxford accent, complete with the slight stutter. I assumed that his son, Saira's heartthrob, was the same. We were both busy, but he seemed rather flattered that a senior executive in the bank wanted to sit down with him to discuss his financial strategy and come to his house to do it. He agreed to the meeting, and we agreed that our respective assistants would set it up.

Thirty minutes later, my assistant, Mildred, came into my office and told me that she had set up the meeting with the Salims for Monday afternoon the following week. The meeting popped up on my online calendar on my desktop and on my phone. I thanked Mildred, and she withdrew.

I texted Roxy for Saira's phone number, but she did not respond till Friday morning. I immediately tapped it in, and Saira picked up on the second ring.

"Yes," she said.

"I'd like to speak to Saira Khan," I said.

"This is Saira. Hello, Hancock."

"I've got an appointment with Mr. Salim for Monday at three in the afternoon. We should meet about thirty minutes before."

"Where should we meet?"

"Let's meet in the lobby of the Mayfair Hotel. It's a short walk from there, and the hotel is easy to find."

"I'll be there," she said.

"And get your brother to open an account with us and deposit the money before the end of business today. If he brings cash, I can make sure that it gets credited right away."

"I'll tell him," she said, hanging up before I could say anything further.

I went back to work and kept at it straight through lunch. My desk phone rang in the early afternoon.

"Excuse me, Mr. Hancock, this is Peter Sanders, down in customer service. I have some gentlemen with me led by a Mr. Hamid Khan, who are trying to make a rather unusual deposit. They mentioned your name as a sponsor. Could you please come down, sir?"

I took the elevator down to the ground floor and went into the retail banking offices. The receptionist directed me to one of the personal banking meeting rooms. I knocked and entered. Peter Sanders, a sandy-haired twenty-something customer service agent, sat at the head of the small conference table with three Pakistani men seated around it. All four of them rose when I walked in.

"Mr. Hancock, thank you for coming down," said Peter. He pointed at a shopping bag on the tabletop. "They have over a hundred thousand pounds in small notes in that bag. They mentioned your name, so I thought it best to call you."

"Thank you, Peter," I said. "It was wise of you to call me. Better safe than sorry."

I pulled up a chair and sat down, waving them all to be seated.

"Which one of you is Hamid Khan?"

"I am," said one of the Pakistanis. His skin was a bit darker than Saira's, but I could see the family resemblance. I pulled the bag toward me and looked in. It was filled with wads of five, ten, and twenty pound notes.

"How did you come by this money?" I asked.

"Restaurants, minicabs, and off-licenses," said Hamid. "We run mostly cash businesses."

"Do you have any documentation?"

"I have brought the accounts of some of our businesses."

He pushed a dog-eared paper file toward me. I opened it and went through it. It was filled with receipts and clipped sheets of accounts in an old-fashioned double entry format. I read through all of them quickly and did some quick mental computations.

"This looks in order," I said. "Mr. Sanders, you can go ahead and open a new investment account for these gentlemen. Sweep all the funds into a money market account for now."

"Yes, sir," said Sanders.

I turned to Hamid. "The interest rate is low, but a money market account is totally safe."

"It better be," he replied.

* * *

13

Friday wound down, and many of the analysts began to leave by three in the afternoon. The traders stayed on, hectically adjusting their positions. Half an hour before market close, I interrupted my work on emails and memo drafting and switched my attention to the big trading screens on my desk. I watched the traders as they unwound their temporary positions and cashed them out for the end of the week. Each trader's activity reflected the overall strategy for the quarter and was supposed to fit in like a jigsaw piece. I saw a few opportunities and sent suggestions to individual traders through the chat boxes.

The market closed, and traders all shut down their terminals, heading for the elevators. By five thirty, the floor was almost deserted. I worked on, losing track of time. My desk phone rang, bringing me back into the present. I glanced at the time on my computer screen before picking up the handset. It was seven thirty.

"Hello, Mr. Hancock," said Roxy. "I finished my first week at Bain Jennings."

"How did it go?"

"Oh, Mr. Hancock, it was unbelievable!" She was so excited that her words tumbled out in a rush. Her accent rapidly became much stronger, and I had to strain to understand her. "It was *so* different doing real trades instead of exercises. I did all the background work for Mr. Bain's bond deals. And he gave me a small mixed portfolio of bonds and equities to trade on me own, and I did ever so well! At the market close today, he cashed out the profits on me mixed portfolio and gave me the money, nearly a thousand quid! And a gold star sticker for me bond work! He said it was what teachers give good students in America."

"I'm so happy for you, Roxy," I said, feeling the tiredness lift from my shoulders.

"Mr. Hancock, we have to celebrate! It would never have happened without you. I'm a rich girl now. I have this money burning a hole in me pocket. I want to take you out tonight."

"Okay, Roxy. Where do you want to go?"

"I've made a reservation, but it's a surprise. I'll come by and pick you up in fifteen minutes. I'll be in the motorbike parking stripes."

"I'll be waiting in the lobby," I said.

*   *   *

14

Roxy had made a booking at an Argentinian steak house in Canary Wharf, right on the river. It was very close to my flat, and I had eaten there before. I thought it was rather overpriced, and that the menu was unnecessarily pretentious. However, I was touched that she was willing to spend her hard-earned money on me and complimented her warmly on her choice. She asked me to order the wine, and I selected a nice little mid-priced Malbec. However, she refused to accept this and accused me of trying to save her money by being cheap. She insisted that I select a Grand Cru, so I reluctantly ordered a Clos de la Roche that I normally would have only ordered if the bank was paying.

Without a doubt, this was the most enjoyable evening of my life. With her blue eyes shining, Roxy was so happy that she lit up the whole room. Her childlike glee warmed my heart. She was everything to me, lover, companion, confidante, best friend. We talked about anything and everything—finance, politics, friendship, love, the philosophy of life and of death. She seemed to be as happy with me as I was with her. It seemed a miracle that this sexy desirable girl-child could actually want to spend time with me.

The Friday night crowd was loud and raucous. It had a truly Argentinian flavor, and people were still arriving at ten, standing around by the bar and waiting for tables. At ten thirty, a tango band arrived and began to warm up. The waiters cleared a dance floor under the direction of a couple of professional dancers. When the band was ready, the male dancer went to the mike, announced his name and that of his lissome partner. She stood by, looking fashionably bored.

The band was quite good—as good as many I had heard in Buenos Aires. The dancers were excellent, far better than I expected. I watched them with rapt attention and did not see Roxy leaving. When I finally noticed, I assumed that she had gone to the ladies' room. She finally returned, beaming from ear to ear, carrying a pair of black high-heeled tango slippers with silver heel cups and ankle straps.

"Where on earth did you get those?" I asked, flabbergasted.

"I asked the waitresses, and one of them told me that the professional couple that dances later tonight is at the bar. I asked the female dancer if I could borrow her shoes, and here they are!"

She changed out of her motorcycle boots into the tango shoes. It was remarkable what this small alteration in her outfit did to her appearance. Her bared fishnet stockings heightened the appeal of her shapely legs, her leather skirt and black silk top seemed to gain elegance, and the heels made her hips swing as she walked.

"Are you going to dance with the male dancer?"

"Of course not, silly. I'm going to dance with you."

"I haven't had a dance lesson in twenty years, Roxy, and tango was never my forte," I protested. "You'd be much better off with—"

"You did very well at Forty-forty."

"Tango is complicated! I barely remember anything."

"Nonsense. The tango hold is so much tighter. We can make it work."

She would not take no for an answer. So when the professionals finished their exhibition and called the public to the floor, we were among the first couples to take our places. The band struck up "El Día Que Me Quieras," one of the best-known tangos and fortunately, one of the easier ones. Roxy knew what she was doing, and after a few false steps, I was moving competently but stiffly across the floor. Most of the couples around us were better than us, but we were not the worst pair. This gave me comfort. As I loosened up, we danced better, and the enjoyment of holding her close grew. I began to see why tango is called the most sensual of dances. Holding her so close, with her body moving tightly against mine, I had a hard time keeping my desire from showing.

We danced set after set, and I lost myself in the music, the movement, and her. Her face radiated so much joy that it amplified my own. Finally, the band took a break, and the cuckoo clock above the bar chimed midnight.

"Let's go home," she said.

That she referred to my place as home was the perfect apex to the evening. She took off the tango shoes and returned them on our way out. She parked her Ducati in the underground car park of my building, and we took the elevator up to my flat on the top floor. She took off her motorcycle boots and jacket in the entrance hallway, and I took her into my arms and kissed her. She kissed me back with aggressive fervor. I picked her up and carried her to the king-size bed in the master bedroom.

"You're getting to be quite an animal, Mr. Hancock," she whispered.

Afterward, she cuddled in my arms, and I held her tight. I wanted the night to never end.

We slept. My internal clock did not turn off on weekends, so I woke before dawn. She was still sleeping in my arms. She looked so little, so young, so vulnerable that I felt fiercely protective. Then she moved to adjust her position, and I kissed her nose, tasting the metal of her nose ring. Her eyes were still glazed with sleep, but she murmured, "Make love to me, Mr. Hancock."

*   *   *

15

Saturday dawned gray and drizzly. We lazed in bed till midmorning. Roxy finally got up and explored the flat, padding around from room to room, running her fingers over the marble countertops, bouncing on the leather sofas and chairs, and looking out the large picture windows at the views of the river and the City towers.

"This is a palace, Mr. Hancock! How can you afford it?"

"The bank is paying for it," I said. "It's probably a long lease, works out cheaper than having me stay at a hotel."

"I've never stayed in such a lovely flat."

"Move in with me," I said. I kept my tone light, but I hoped. "There's more. The gym downstairs is nice, there's a pool on the roof, and there's a club room with billiards, table tennis, and a half decent library."

"Hmmm, a tempting offer," she said. "Will they take Alfie?"

"I can ask."

"Hungry?" she asked, abruptly changing the subject.

"Starving," I said.

"I'll make breakfast. I'm the egg queen."

She went to kitchen and pulled out everything I had in the fridge and put it on the island. I pulled on a robe and watched her slicing peppers, tomatoes, and onions with one of the super sharp chef's knives from the block. She made a very fluffy Western omelet with brown toast and coffee. Then she laid the table in the breakfast nook to perfection, plates, quarter plates, knives, forks, spoons, and glasses in their classic place settings. She poured out the orange juice and indicated the table with a flourish.

"Your breakfast is served, m'lord," she said.

I came up behind her and put my arms around her.

"I don't know which hunger to sate first," I said.

"The omelet will get cold," she said, giggling. "But I'll stay hot."

I sat across from her in the breakfast nook and concentrated on the omelet and toast. It was no idle boast—the omelet was indeed excellent, cooked just so, with the vegetables tender but not limp.

"I'm going to take a shower, then go to see Danny and Harry again," she said after we ate. "Weekends are always depressing in the hospital."

"How do you know?" I began, but then I remembered her violent childhood, and my voice trailed off.

*   *   *

16

She left around noon, promising to come back later in the evening. I went online and bought tickets to an evening Mozart concert at St. Martin-in-the-Fields to surprise her. Then I went back to work, drafting memos, editing strategy documents, and reading global reports of economic trends.

By two in the afternoon, my eyes were getting heavy, so I stood up, stretched, and did a slow five-mile jog on the treadmill in the gym. Showered and changed, I felt more energized and decided to have a coffee before returning to work. I went downstairs, walked a few blocks to my usual gourmet coffee shop, and returned to the lobby of my building, sipping a latte.

"Got a minute, Hancock?"

Nick materialized by my side, seemingly from nowhere. He put a hand on my shoulder, and I felt his powerful fingers through my jacket and shirt. He wore a motorcycle outfit—Kevlar-braced leather jacket, pants, and boots. His expression was neutral, but I started guiltily.

"Sure," I said.

"Me motorbike's outside. Let's take a ride."

It did not look like I had a choice in the matter. He assumed that I would obey him and did not look around. He walked up to a red Ducati, and I said, "Is that Roxy's bike?"

"No, hers is a twin of mine," he said. "I bought it for her when she started working at your bank in the City."

"She's an incredible rider," I said.

"I know," he replied. "I taught her."

The two helmets clipped onto brackets were also identical to Roxy's. I took the rear one, put it on, and climbed on behind Nick. It was uncomfortable, for I held his shoulders gingerly, unwilling to get into a close clasp with him. He seemed to understand and rode quite sedately, threading his way through traffic, heading east. Once we got into the East End, he made his way through a maze of alleys, recalling my ride with Roxy to meet Saira. But these were different—a postindustrial landscape of derelict factories and warehouses, interspersed with small islands of drab terraced houses. Gentrification had clearly not reached this part of the East End. Eventually, he pulled up in front of the pub where I had met Roxy before—The Wheatsheaf.

He set the motorbike on its kickstand. We clipped the helmets to it and entered the pub together. Several tough looking men nodded to Nick, their expressions deferential. Nick went to a table that was set by itself, off in the corner and seated himself. He indicated another chair, as though he was giving me permission to sit. I did so.

Before he could speak, Tilly came up, sat on his lap, and put her arms around him possessively. She was wearing a skirt so short that it could have been hidden by a ballet tutu. Her thin silk blouse had ruffled sleeves that she had pushed down to reveal her shoulders and ruffles over her breasts. She rubbed herself on Nick like a cat.

"Hancock, I'm having the real ale," said Nick. "What do you want?"

"I'll have the same," I said.

"Tilly luv, get us beers, will you?"

"I'm not a barmaid!" she said petulantly.

She stood up, smoothed her skirt, and tossed her head, showing off the bounce of her striking mane of auburn hair. Then, in spite of her declaration, she went to the bar.

"Tilly's gorgeous," I said.

"Yes, she looks like a million quid. And she's great in bed. But she's a great pain out of it, clingy, whiny. She loves the status of being my number one girl and doesn't care who else I see, as long as they don't challenge her. So different from Roxy, who doesn't care about status but is as jealous as a cat."

Tilly returned with the beers, set them down, and prepared to seat herself on Nick's lap again. However, he slapped her bottom and said, "Give us some time alone, sweetheart. I have some business to discuss with Hancock."

She ruffled his hair before walking back to the bar, clicking her high heels, and swinging her hips a bit more the necessary. She got the eye of every man in the bar except the one whose attention she sought.

"Come with me," he said, picking up his beer and standing up.

I picked up my beer, and he nudged me toward the fire exit at the rear of the bar. He ignored the "alarm will sound" sign and pushed it open. Outside was a small dingy patio, overhung with an awning and opening into a narrow alley that led out to a side street. There was a cement block table, surrounded by old planked benches. It faced solid brick walls all around.

"No one will hear us here," he said.

"I'm not sure that makes me feel better," I replied.

"Did Roxy tell you how I met her?" he asked, ignoring my response.

It was clear from Nick's expression that he wanted to tell me, so I said nothing and waited for him to go on.

"It was not far from here. I was headed here to the Wheatsheaf, actually, when the door to one of the terraced houses was thrown open, and this little seven year old comes running out, screaming, 'No, no, no!' She runs right into me and falls down on the pavement. It's a freezing December day, and she's in her underwear. This heavyset bloke comes rushing out after her with a butcher knife in one hand and a hardon in the other. He stops short when he sees me. 'Oh hi, Nick,' he says to me with a leer. 'Why don't we share her? You can go first.' She gets up off the pavement but just stands there, shivering, looking at me like a frightened kitten. She doesn't run. She's given up, you see."

He took a swig of his beer and set down the glass, carefully placing it on a coaster. He was not looking at me but over my shoulder, into the distance. His lips trembled, and his eyes were soft, like he was on the verge of tears.

"That's how Roxy grew up, Hancock. Seven years old and she honestly thought that I was going to join this filthy pig and gang rape her. That's what she expected from the world."

"What did you do?"

"What do you think? I got Roxy a blanket, then beat the stuffin' out of the bloke. Later, I took her shoppin'. 'Buy anythin' you want, darlin',' I said to her. 'Anythin' in the high street, it's yours.' I'll never forget the stars in her eyes. It cost me seven quid, two for a doll and five for a pink dress, both from the charity shop. It was the only shop in the high street that she'd ever been in. She was too frightened to go anywhere else."

He paused, then shook his head, as though he was returning from that day.

"Her mum died. I took her to live with me and watched her grow up. She was my little girl. I wanted her to be perfect! I made her go to school, the same one I went to. I went to every parent event and made sure the teachers knew she had someone who cared about her at home."

A school that the government rates as failing, I thought. But I did not say anything.

"I paid for dance lessons, kickboxing, and karate. I got her into bicycle racing, taught her to ride a motorbike. She just immersed herself in every opportunity that I gave her, soaked it all in. I don't know how that crackhead mum of hers produced this girl. She's not like the others around here. Roxy is special, one of a kind."

"You're her Pygmalion."

"Sorry?"

"It's a Greek legend," I said. "Pygmalion was a sculptor who created a marble statue of a beautiful girl and fell in love with the stone figure. Aphrodite, the goddess of love, saw him dressing and embracing the cold stone and took pity on him. She granted his wish and brought the statue to life, a girl called Galatea." I paused to drink my beer. "You made her. Now you've fallen in love with her."

"Yes, Hancock, I fell in love with her. I still love her. Madly."

He drank again, then reached into his jacket, produced a zippered leather case and put it on the cement block surface.

"Open it."

I opened the zipper halfway around and saw the butt of the gun. I'm no gun nut, but it looked like a Glock. He grasped the butt but did not pull it out of the leather case.

I felt my knees begin to quake, but fortunately they were out of sight under the table. I looked into Nick's eyes but did not see bloodlust there, only hurt. I put my hands together on the table and thought of Roxy in my arms, dancing the tango.

"Roxy told me she wants you to help her get established in the City. Are you sleeping with her?"

"Yes. But she told me it's just sex."

"Roxy's my girl, Hancock," he said. "I want you out of her life. One way or the other."

"Are you going to shoot me here? And lose everything you've worked for all your life?"

"Why would I lose anything? Do you think anyone in there is going to squeal on me?" He jerked his thumb indicating the interior of the pub. "A bit of quick-setting cement, a short trip to the Thames, a small splash in the middle of the river in the dark of night—and you'll never be found. 'Banker plagued by scandal disappears.' A few days in the interior pages of the papers, then forgotten. Who's going to miss you Hancock?"

"No one," I said. *Dolores will get my life insurance after they declare me legally dead*, I thought. *I wish there was some way I could give it to Roxy.* Last night and this morning were the happiest times of my life. What better time to end it?

"Go ahead, shoot me. But that won't get Roxy to come back to you. She said she broke up with you long before she met me."

Nick took his hand off the gun butt and pounded the concrete tabletop.

"I don't understand what she wants!" he cried. "I have money to burn, but she won't take a penny from me. She used to live off the pittance she made as a bicycle messenger. I gave her the Ducati when she moved away, but she insisted on paying me back from her salary at your bank."

"She saw what happened to her mother, Nick. You sell what killed her. She doesn't want the money that comes from that."

"Drugs didn't kill her mum," said Nick. He tapped his temple. "It was something in her head. If it wasn't drugs, it would have been booze, pills, something else. She had this need to escape, and getting high was her way of doing it. Roxy's not as different from her mum as she thinks."

"What do you mean?"

"Have you seen how she rides that motorbike? Every ride is about getting a high, getting somewhere is secondary."

"I know," I said.

Nick covered his face with his hands.

"I made her the princess of the East End, but she didn't want it. All she ever wanted was to get out of here, to escape the place she grew up and the only place that'll accept her. The place where she belongs."

"She'll make it in the City, Nick," I said.

"Those toffs will never accept her, Hancock."

"I can show you a dozen Essex lads and barrow boys who are managing directors and vice presidents in the City, Nick."

"She's a bird, Hancock. Those barrow boys who've made it are more sexist than the real toffs. They try even harder to fit in. It's hard enough for a respectable girl. No one will give a bird like Roxy a break." He drained his beer mug. "Her boss, your upper-class American girl, was happy to use Roxy's contacts out here, getting girls and drugs to grease the wheels of her deals. But she didn't want her to study, did she? Roxy came right back here after she got the sack. She was crying her eyes out. Maggie told me."

"I didn't know that," I said unhappily. "I thought Roxy was tough—"

"She's got a tough shell. But inside, she's as soft as a pudding." He zipped the leather gun case closed. "She'll try hard, Hancock. She'll work till blood runs from her eyes. Roxy never does anything by half measures, and she can do anything she puts her mind to. But those toffs in the City won't let her succeed."

I opened my mouth to tell Nick about Roxy's job at Bain Jennings, but then I shut it again.

"And when she finally realizes that she can't make it there, she'll come back to me. But in the meantime, take care of my Roxy, Hancock. Don't let them hurt her. And go back to sleeping with your American girl, she's more your type. Like Roxy is mine."

*   *   *

17

The meeting with Nick cast a shadow over my mood leading into the perfect Saturday evening I'd planned with Roxy. Things went downhill from there, more so because I had set my expectations so high. Roxy was polite during the Mozart concert, but it was clear that she did not enjoy it. Afterward, I took her to a Japanese restaurant that I particularly liked, but she ate sparingly. She did not like sake at all, so I ordered her Japanese beer that she likened to piss. After I settled the check, she decided that she wanted to spend the night at her place, saying that Alfie was missing her. She dropped me at my place, and I watched her bright taillight disappear down the road. I went up to my flat feeling very depressed. I went straight to bed, but I kept thinking of Roxy and couldn't sleep. I finally got up, poured myself a large single malt scotch, and fell asleep in an armchair in the living room.

I got up at dawn on Sunday, stiff and sore. I pulled on a robe and made myself some coffee. I sipped it and read the Asian financial pages on my laptop to distract myself. Around eight thirty, my phone rang. I looked at the screen and was surprised to see Saira's colorful profile picture. I tapped it open, wondering why she was calling so early in the morning.

"Hancock, I've arranged with my parents for you to visit us today. I'll send you our address. Be here by half past twelve."

"Wait, wait," I said, realizing that she was about to hang up. "What's going on? Why am I coming?"

"You met Hamid at the bank on Friday, right?"

"Yes," I said. "The account is online and functioning. I tested it. Everything works. There's no need to meet."

"That's not what this is about." She sounded impatient. "When we go to the Salims tomorrow, you're going to pretend to be a friend of my family. We better build some evidence for that."

"I don't know what to say to your parents," I said.

"Just make small talk."

I got a taxi about eleven thirty and arrived at the address that Saira sent me fifteen minutes early. It was long row of terraced houses, neat and well-maintained, quite at odds with the shabby homes in the rest of the neighborhood and even across the street. There were several tough-looking young men out in the street, and they closed in behind me as I approached the address she had sent me. I tried to ignore them and rang the bell.

Hamid opened the door, and at his signal, the young toughs dispersed. He wore jeans and a muscle shirt that displayed his robust upper body. He did not greet me but led me down a narrow entrance hallway to a sitting room. The furniture and fittings were high quality, but there was too much gilt and gold paint for my taste. There was a very large flat-screen TV playing a song and dance routine featuring large numbers of garishly clothed dancers. The volume was loud and assaulted my ears with the pounding drumbeat.

"Tea?" he asked, gesturing to plush armchair in a corner facing the TV.

"Yes, thank you," I said, sitting down.

Saira's parents entered along with a maid, who brought in a tray with cups of tea and biscuits. She set the tray down on the large coffee table at the center of the room and left. Saira came in a few moments later. She was dressed much more formally than when I had met her with Roxy. She wore a much more lavish shalwar kameez with a *dupatta* that had gold filigree worked into it. She draped it over her head and shoulders in the manner of her mother. Her parents and brother brightened appreciably on her entrance. The way all three of them looked at her made it clear how much she was treasured. I just could not understand how this love could induce them to kill her for sleeping with a man.

I began a rather uncomfortable conversation about the weather, but Saira's father quickly turned it to the extent to which prominent families of Pakistani origin banked with us. He brought up the Salims, and I tried to imply a connection to them without actually lying. Hamid asked whether I would vouch for his family's financial good standing. I managed to say enough to keep them satisfied without committing to anything formal.

I stayed for a decorous hour and then took my leave. Hamid walked me out, and there was one of his minicabs waiting to take me back to my flat.

*   *   *

18

On Monday, I waited for Saira in the lobby of the Mayfair Hotel, doing some work on my laptop. The concierge recognized me and came up to ask if I wanted anything.

"I'm waiting for a Ms. Khan, Albert," I said. "Do show her to me when she comes."

Five minutes later, he brought Saira to me. She was wearing the red and gold lamé sari she had mentioned with the *pallu* wrapped around her and over her head, covering her upper body and her hair. She wore gold bangles, and there was low-key melodious tinkling when she walked. She smoothed the folds of her sari, sat down in a facing chair, and Albert politely withdrew. I saw that the tinkling came from silver anklets that had small bells on them. They were worn over the straps of delicate high-heeled silver slippers. Painstakingly made up and exquisitely turned out, she was stunning and drew curious looks from all around the lobby. Even Albert broke with protocol and sneaked a glance back over his shoulder for another look at her.

"You look beautiful, Saira," I said. "And very traditional. I'm sure the Salims will be impressed."

"There's no need to flatter me, Hancock. As soon as I open my mouth, they'll know that I'm just an East End girl." She took in my Savile Row banker's pinstripe suit, understated Italian designer tie, platinum monogrammed cufflinks, and the mirrorlike polish of my wingtips. "You're dressed up as well."

"Do your parents allow you to travel about London alone, all dressed up like this?"

"One of our minicabs dropped me off. I'll call for one to take me back later."

We walked down the lanes together and emerged on to Park Lane. The doorman at the Salims' building was grandly dressed with a top hat and frock coat. He opened the door for us with a flourish. Saira looked back over her shoulder at him as we walked into the lobby. The man at the reception desk was also impeccably turned out with a spotless white shirt, black tie, and jacket with red pips on the lapels.

"Mr. Hancock and Ms. Khan for Mr. Salim," I said.

"Just a moment, sir," he said.

He called the flat and a moment later, waved us to the bank of elevators. The Salims had the penthouse that occupied the top two floors. The door was opened by a liveried butler, who conducted us to a large book-lined study with a wide window that overlooked Hyde Park. I glanced at Saira and saw that her eyes were wide. This world was clearly foreign to her. I found her awestruck expression endearing. *She's an East End princess like Roxy*, I thought. *But a foreigner in the West End.*

The butler returned a few minutes later.

"Mr. and Mrs. Shaheed Khan Salim," he announced.

The Salims' appearance was quite at odds with the grand mode of their entrance. Mr. Salim wore a suit, tie, and accessories that were at least as expensive as mine, and Mrs. Salim wore a gold brocaded sari with subtle but fine gold jewelry. But he was short, dark, and stout; she was much paler but also quite short. He bustled in, looking like an overdressed shopkeeper. Only his bright hooded eyes gave a clue as to his intellectual acumen. His wife followed him in and allowed him to take charge of the proceedings.

I stood up and bent forward to be on his level to shake hands.

"Welcome, welcome, Mr. Hancock," he said. His handshake was firm, and he looked me directly in the eye. He was an old Etonian, and it showed. "I am flattered that you have set up a meeting in my abode and made it so convenient for me. Perhaps, I should transfer more of my business to your bank."

"We will endeavor to serve you to the best of our abilities, Mr. Salim," I said, smiling. "Regardless of the quantity of business you do with us."

"I am sure you will," he said.

Saira had stood up as well, but she remained mute with downcast eyes as befitted a modest South Asian woman. She adjusted her *pallu*, making sure that her hair was fully covered. I saw that both the Salims were looking at her with polite interest, waiting for me to introduce her.

"Mr. and Mrs. Salim, this is Ms. Saira Khan. I'm an old family friend and ran into her with her brother, Hamid, having tea at the Mayfair Hotel. Hamid had some urgent business to attend to, so he asked me to be her chaperone and take her back to her home in the East End. I hope you do not mind my trespassing on your hospitality like this."

"Not at all," said Mrs. Salim, speaking up before her husband could respond. Her accent was distinctly provincial and sounded from the north of England. "We are always happy to entertain well-bred young people." She turned to Saira. "I love your sari, my dear. You must tell me where you got it."

"Thank you, Auntie," said Saira, speaking from under downcast eyes. She fluttered her eyelashes, and it quickened my pulse. I glanced over at Mr. Salim and saw that he noticed her too. "My mother bought it for me some months ago. It was for my cousin Humaira's *nikah*."

"Your cousin, Humaira," said Mrs. Salim with increased interest. "What is her full name? Where is she from?"

"Humaira Siddiqui, Auntie. She grew up in Bradford."

"Why, she is my cousin's daughter! My family is from Bradford. They still live there. Mr. Salim and I were out of the country, otherwise, I would have certainly come to her *nikah*! I sent our son, Iftekhar, to represent us."

Saira remained quiet, still looking down at her feet. It was a contrast to her behavior at our earlier meeting, but she looked so genuine that I could not tell whether she was pretending or in earnest.

"So we are related!" said Mrs. Khan. "Where did you grow up, *beti*?"

"Tower Hamlets, Auntie."

"Do you speak Urdu?"

"Yes, Auntie."

Mrs. Salim let loose a barrage of words, and I could not understand a single one. Saira responded fluently but spoke slowly and in a low tone. I shot a look at Mr. Salim. He seemed almost as lost as I was.

They spoke for a few minutes before Mrs. Salim stopped and addressed her husband.

"Why don't Saira and I take our tea over in the sun room? That way, we will not interfere with your business meeting with Mr. Hancock."

"What a good idea, my dear," said Mr. Salim.

Mrs. Salim conducted Saira out, and I heard her as they passed through the door. "It is such good fortune that Mr. Hancock brought you over, *beti*. I have heard of your family, of course, but you are so different from what I expected."

A maid brought in tea and cakes, and I sat down with Mr. Salim. I had badgered the high net worth asset management team to get his portfolio with us and brought it up on my laptop. I went over my suggestions for a strategic reallocation that would move its balance toward Asian markets. He asked intelligent questions, making me thankful that I had prepared well. It took over an hour to go over it all.

"So," I concluded, "to implement this strategy, it will require some additional investments, but I hope I have convinced you that the expected returns justify the additional risk."

"Almost," he said. "I'm a bit less sanguine than you are about the risk in some of these emerging markets."

"I think we can arrange to build in some insurance," I said. "We have a range of complementary instruments that will reduce the risk."

"No doubt they will cost me money," he groused.

I thought of Roxy's admonition, "A few beeps on a corporate bond issue."

"Given the size of your investment, we can ensure that the complementary instruments are, in fact, complimentary."

I smiled at my pun, but he did not.

"You would lower my risk for free?"

"In short, yes, Mr. Salim."

His mood improved noticeably, and he chatted amiably about the state of the London property market, while we helped ourselves to cakes and sipped our tea.

"So tell me about this Hamid Khan," he said suddenly. "How do you know the family? Surely they are not typical of your friends? Saira talks like an East End shop girl."

"We've been trying to break into the Pakistani community for some time," I said, ignoring his comment about Saira's accent. "They run a lot of cash-intensive businesses, and I've long felt that there's huge untapped potential there. If we can help them securitize their assets, we can build a huge superstructure of financial value on the foundation of all that cash. It's a win-win. We can make money, and the community can get rich. Doing well by doing good, as it were." I paused to see how he was taking this. He didn't look convinced, so I went on. "A connection to the less fortunate minorities in the East End is also good PR for the bank. It will make us look good to the politicians. The director of our London operation is building his case for a peerage."

This got through to him, for I saw the interest flare up in his eyes for a moment. But it came and went in an instant.

"The trouble is that they've been burned by a lot shysters over the years, so they don't trust bankers. They think we're a bunch of greedy bloodsuckers. But I've finally managed to get Hamid to make an initial deposit with us. I'm confident it will be the first of many."

I sipped my tea, and he sipped his.

"Hamid Khan is reputed to be one of the biggest drug dealers in London. He's been linked to gang activity."

"I've gone over some of his accounts personally," I said carefully. "He and his family run restaurants, minicabs, and shops. They have quite a healthy cash flow. You know how it is. Any Pakistani in the East End who has money is assumed to run drugs and participate in gang activity."

"Hmm, I suppose so," he said grudgingly. "I've been accused of drug running myself on occasion."

Mrs. Salim and Saira returned, along with a young man that I assumed was the son, Iftekhar.

"Hello, Dad," Iftekhar said. He had an Oxford accent like his father. "Mum and I just had tea with Saira."

They all came in and sat down.

"Shaheed," said Mrs. Salim. "Saira and I have just spent a delightful hour together. It does my heart good to speak in Urdu. She speaks it so well and such a nice accent too. There's no pretense about her, unlike so many of our girls born here in England. I wish Iftekhar and you would take the trouble to learn our languages."

"I understand enough," said Mr. Salim.

"And so do I," said Iftekhar. "Though I would like to improve. Perhaps Saira can help me."

"Shaheed, I have invited Saira to stay for dinner," said Mrs. Salim, smiling at her son's remark. "But she says she cannot possibly do so without her chaperone. So you must prevail on Mr. Hancock to stay."

I thought of the mountain of work that was piling up in the office and was about to politely decline, but Mr. Salim forestalled me.

"A good idea, Mr. Hancock," he said. "That will give us time to discuss some ideas I've been having about REITs."

Given the size of the Salims' property holdings, I could not ignore this opportunity. The high net worth asset management team would owe me for this.

"Let me call my office and make a few arrangements for this afternoon's work," I said. "Then I am your man."

*   *   *

19

The rest of the week passed slowly. I met Roxy every morning at the coffee shop in Coleman Street to go over her preparations for the financial markets exams. They were only days away now, at the end of the week. She was getting nervous, no matter how many times I told her that she would find the test quite easy. She also brought me news of Saira.

"Saira and you were a hit, Mr. Hancock," she said. "You turned out to be the perfect team. Mrs. Salim just fell in love with Saira."

"Well, Mrs. Salim seemed to really enjoy talking to her in Urdu."

"Yes, it turns out that they have lots of relatives in common. She's already pushing her husband to think of Saira as a bride for Iftekhar. She's arranged to meet Saira's mum. A few more weeks and I think they'll be engaged."

"You should have seen her, Roxy. Dressed in that red and gold sari with bangles and anklets, she looked gorgeous, like something out of a magazine. And she played the modest demure maiden very well. She covered her hair, wrapped herself in the sari so only her face showed. And she had these tiny bells on her anklets that jingled as she walked." I paused to take a breath. "I was totally convinced that it was all real."

Roxy laughed out loud.

"She was always good at acting like butter wouldn't melt in her mouth. Did she bat her eyelashes?"

"Yes!" I exclaimed. "With downcast eyes. She even captured Mr. Salim's attention when she did that."

"I told you, she's a pro, Mr. Hancock. If she wanted to seduce you, you wouldn't last an hour."

"She could never seduce me," I said firmly. "I'm spoken for."

"By who? Your wife is in the process of divorcing you. You're a free man."

"But…but…" I stammered, "you and me—"

"Oh, we have an arrangement," she said, patting my cheek. "But I wouldn't dream of tying you down."

After she left to go to Bain Jennings, I sat in the coffee shop for another half an hour, too depressed to go to work.

*　　*　　*

20

The financial markets exams were on Saturday, and I texted Roxy that I would meet her at the test center an hour before the start. Roxy arrived looking very nervous and rather pale, even for her. I took her to a coffee shop. She looked unfocused as she sipped her cappuccino.

"Relax," I said. "You're well prepared. You'll do very well. Just go over each question thoroughly before you put down your answer."

"I haven't had an exam in years, Mr. Hancock."

Nonetheless, the coffee seemed to calm her. She gripped my hand just before entering the exam hall.

"I'm not feeling very well, Mr. Hancock," she said.

"Probably just nerves," I said. "You'll be fine once you start. I'll be waiting right here."

I sat in the foyer. It was a three-hour exam, and now that she was in it, I was nervous. I really hoped she would do well, but I told myself that I would be satisfied if she just passed and got the qualification.

About an hour passed slowly. Then the big old doors to the hall opened, and Roxy came out, along with a female invigilator.

"What's the matter?" I asked, unnerved. I quickly went to her side.

"I feel like I want to puke, Mr. Hancock," Roxy said.

"She can have five minutes," said the invigilator, an elderly woman with a starchy demeanor. She did not look pleased with Roxy's appearance or with her accent.

I followed them to the ladies' toilet and waited outside. Minutes ticked by, and eventually, I grew so impatient and worried that I opened the door and went in.

"Sir, really!" cried the invigilator. "This is outrageous! Are you some kind of pervert?"

Roxy was doubled over the sink, retching. There was some evidence of vomiting in the bowl, but mostly she was racked with dry heaves. I came to her side and put one hand on her neck to steady her, rubbing her back with the other. The invigilator retired to a safe distance in high dudgeon, but I did not pay her any further attention.

"Take your time," I said to Roxy. "It will pass. Here, take this. Sucking on these may help."

I gave her the box of breath mints that I always carried in my pocket. The heaving finally subsided, and she rinsed her face and mouth. She stood up and leaned on me. She looked weak, but she took the box of breath mints.

"How do you feel?" I asked.

"Not great," she confessed. "But better." She popped a breath mint in her mouth. "I better get back to the exam before she disbars me."

All three of us left the ladies' together. Roxy and the invigilator went back into the exam hall, while I resumed my seat outside. Time seemed to pass even slower now, especially since I knew Roxy was not feeling well. I stood up and paced. I knew that there were emails piling up in my inbox that I should probably respond to on my phone, but I could not think about work now.

Finally, the heavy doors to the exam hall were pushed open, and the first exam takers began emerging. I asked a few of them how the exam was, but their responses were noncommittal. In a way, I was happy that Roxy had not come out yet because I hoped that she was taking the exam seriously and checking her work. The three hours were finally up, and I heard a general bustle from within the exam hall. The heavy doors were pushed open, set on their chocks, and the mass of exam takers streamed out. Roxy was one of the last to come out. She looked ill.

"How are you feeling?" I asked, the exam driven out of my mind.

"Not too good," she said. "I need to go to the loo again."

I could not accompany her this time, for there were many women in there. I waited outside anxiously. Finally, she came out, looking tired and wan.

"What happened?" I asked.

"I started feeling bad early this morning," she replied. "It woke me up before dawn. I was nauseous, and me tits were tingling and sore."

We walked out of the building, and she walked around the back to the two-wheeler parking stripes.

"Aren't you going to wait for the exam results?"

"I need to do another exam." She put her helmet without saying anything further.

I grabbed the second helmet and put it on.

"You want to come along?" It was odd to suddenly transition to her metallic sounding voice through the Bluetooth link.

"Yes," I said.

"You don't know where I'm going."

"I just want to be with you, Roxy. Especially since you're not feeling well."

She did not reply but let me climb aboard the motorbike behind her. I held on tightly, and she gunned the machine out of the narrow alley. She headed east, cutting through the lighter weekend traffic at high speed. I was used to her now, but every now and then, she cut around a vehicle or traffic island so close that my clothing brushed it, and I involuntarily tightened my hold on her. We passed Aldgate East tube station, and very soon afterward, she pulled into a side street and parked. We walked into a narrow mews, and she rang an electric bell at a door next to a loading dock whose rolling shutter was down and locked. The intercom by the bell crackled to life, and I could just make out a voice through the static, "Who is it?"

"Roxy, here for Penny," she said.

The door buzzed, and Roxy pushed it open. We walked down a dimly lit corridor whose walls were once white but had faded to a rather dull shade of cream. I guessed it was a medical establishment, and this was confirmed when we passed a noticeboard that identified it as a clinic. Shortly thereafter, we got to a reception desk.

"Penny's got someone with her," the girl at the reception said to Roxy. "But she said to tell you to come straight in. She's in room 4, fourth door on your right."

She pointed down the corridor behind her. There were several people waiting outside room 4, some on a bench and some standing. The door was of frosted glass with the numeral "4" on it. Roxy pushed it open and went it. I made to follow her, but she spoke over her shoulder, saying, "Wait outside, Mr. Hancock."

I joined the other people, disappointed. It was a mixed crowd of Pakistanis, Afro-Caribbeans, and a few whites. Several people eyed me suspiciously.

"You a copper?" an elderly man asked me, touching my elbow. "We're all good folk here, y' know?"

"No, no, I'm not a policeman," I said.

"American," he said.

"Yes."

"What are you doin' here? Not the best place for a tourist."

I did not reply, hoping he would stop talking to me, and to my relief, he started talking to someone else.

Roxy finally emerged and walked down the corridor without waiting for me or even looking at me. I trotted after her, for she was walking fast. She still did not look at me when I caught up with her. I put on my helmet and mounted the motorbike behind her. She still did not say anything to me, but she did acquiesce my riding with her and holding her.

"Roxy, what's the matter?" I asked when she drove out into traffic.

She did not reply but dived into a roundabout, causing me to cling to her even tighter. She drove to my place in Canary Wharf and screeched to a stop in front of my building. I got off, took off my helmet, and attached it to the bar on her motorbike. I realized that she was about to drive off and leave me, so I held her arm with both hands.

"Roxy, tell me what I've done," I pleaded. "Don't freeze me out."

She put the machine on its kickstand and took off her helmet in silence. But she left the engine running. She put her hands on her hips, both balled into fists. Her eyes flashed. She was very angry.

"You haven't guessed why I'm pissed?" Her voice was like a whiplash. Her harsh accent had never sounded less pleasant.

"I know you're feeling sick, Roxy—"

"I'm not sick, Mr. Hancock," she hissed. She sounded like she hated me. "I'm pregnant, you wanker!"

"I'm so sorry, Roxy," I said. "I'll pay for an abortion."

I spontaneously tried to hug her. As I closed with her, she used her right forearm like a piston and punched me hard. She hit me right between my healing ribs, and I felt like all the wind was sucked out of my body. My mouth formed an "O," but there was only a whistling sound as I exhaled all the air in my lungs. I felt a pain at the base of my spine and realized that I had fallen hard on my tailbone onto the pavement. I saw her swing her foot back and braced myself for the impact of her motorcycle boot. I didn't have time to put up my arms to protect myself.

Her boot stopped a few inches from my face. She didn't kick me. The shock subsided, and I felt the searing pain from my ribs. *They're probably broken again*, I thought. I slowly tipped over sideways, like a ship that's been holed below the waterline. I lay there on the cold concrete, my breath coming in quick gasps. I couldn't move. I watched her go back to her motorbike and put her helmet on again.

She mounted it, flipped up the kickstand, and gunned the engine. I closed my eyes.

I don't know how long I lay there. But I finally heaved myself to my feet, gritting my teeth against the pain. I swayed and took an unsteady step or two. Then I felt a hand grip my forearm and steady me. Roxy put my arm around her shoulders, and we made our way into my building and up to my flat. She lay me down in the master bedroom and sat on the bed beside me.

"I want to help, Roxy," I said. "I know you don't want a child now—"

"Don't mention an abortion unless you want me to hit you again," she threatened. "I'm not doing to this baby what me mum tried to do to me."

"You told me you were on the pill—"

"I am," said Roxy. "But that first weekend at the Taylor Hotel in the Cotswolds, I forgot to take it. I got drunk, and I was ovulating. Penny told me that was a lethal combination—missing the pill, alcohol, and time of the month."

And at twenty, she's near the peak of her fertility, I thought.

She helped me out of my jacket and undid the buttons of my shirt, one at a time. She kissed the injured region very lightly. She caressed my newly rebroken ribs with her fingers.

"I'm sorry for lashing out at you," she whispered. "But this was not supposed to happen. A baby was not part of our deal."

I did not know what to say, so I kept silent. In the evening, I went online to check the exam results. Roxy had been to the bathroom several times during the afternoon to retch over the sink and was lying in bed, exhausted and ill. So I took my laptop there and showed it to her without a word. At the top of the screen, just under the capital markets header next to the gold medal icon was her name—Roxy Reid. She looked at the screen for a moment without a change of expression. Then a slow smile suffused her face.

"Not too shabby, huh?" she said.

"I told you," I said. "And you did it even with your morning sickness."

She rolled over to show me her back. I ran my fingers over her smooth skin, tracing the Chinese characters of the tattoo between her shoulder blades.

"I'm not sure I've taught you anything, Roxy," I said.

"That's exactly what Lao Tzu is saying, Mr. Hancock," she responded, pulling my head down and kissing me. The movement hurt my ribs a great deal, but it was worth it.

*　*　*

21

The next month was a rollercoaster of emotions. Sometimes Roxy was exuberant, and we spent the evenings in laughter and the nights making wild love. Other times, she was withdrawn and did not want to be touched. But worst of all was when she went incommunicado, refusing to respond to my texts, phone messages, and emails, so I had no idea where she was or who she was with. She transitioned from one mood to the other with frightening unpredictability. I did my best to cope.

My own moods began to mirror hers, with bursts of happiness when she was up, despondency when she was down, and deep depression when she dropped out of my life, sometimes for a week and more. Work was unrelenting, and I lost myself in it. I knew she was working long hours as well. Chad called now and again to talk about Roxy.

"She's brilliant, Jim, there's no doubt of that," he said. "I let her run some of her own trades now that she's passed the financial markets exam. But my gosh, she's moody! I just leave her alone, otherwise it's like walking on eggshells. Sometimes she lashes out at the most innocent comment. Other times, she's laughing and joking, bringing in trays of coffee for everyone. But her work is excellent, so I'm not complaining."

* * *

22

My divorce case wound its way forward. The law is a slow process, and I got updates from my lawyer, Bud Brewster, every week. He tried very hard to get Dolores's legal team to agree to a division of our assets, but they were unrelenting. Bud told me that he assumed she was pushing her team. But he assured me he was continuing to negotiate.

Another month went by. Roxy was eight weeks into her pregnancy, and I took her out to dinner. She was in a foul mood and nothing could please her—the food was terrible, the service was worse, and anything I said was met with ridicule or anger. So I withdrew into silence. She was on her phone, and I did not ask her what she was doing with it. My own phone rang, and it was a relief to have something to do other than wait for Roxy's next negative comment. It was Bud Brewster.

"Bud!" I said with false cheerfulness. "Great to hear from you."

"Hi, Jim," he said, sounding particularly morose. "Are you sitting down?"

"Yes," I said. "What's the matter?"

"I won't sugarcoat it, Jim," said Bud. "As you know, I've been going back and forth negotiating with Dolores's legal team. But Dolores met with Logan Baldwin yesterday and gave him the entire dossier. And today, her lawyers called, terminating negotiations. They want everything, or else they'll go to court. They're going to subpoena the child prostitute Dolores caught you with, the one in the photos."

"My god," I said.

"I've called my partners. We're putting together a team to represent you in court. It will be a media circus, but if the prostitute is of age, as you say, we should be able to save a significant chunk of your assets."

"We're not going to court, Bud," I said firmly.

"Jim, Dolores's lawyers made it quite clear that the only way they're settling out of court is if you give her everything. Every last penny."

"Give Dolores everything. But I'm not going to let her drag that girl into court."

There was long pause.

"It's your money, Jim. And your divorce. I'll do whatever you want."

"Thank you, Bud. Send me whatever paperwork is necessary to settle. I'll sign it."

"Okay, Jim. I'll do that. Take care."

The line went dead, and I ended the call. I felt like the bottom had fallen out of my world.

"Another call from the States?" asked Roxy, looking up from her phone.

"Yes," I said gloomily.

"Well, let's go. Me tits are sore, and me nipples are so swollen that I need to take the rings off."

Her mood was so black that I did not share my despair.

*   *   *

23

I got a call from Logan the next day in the midmorning, just about when I expected it. He must have landed early in the morning, gotten a nap, and a shower, and come straight to the office. He had taken over the corner office of the president of the London subsidiary. The receptionist was expecting me, rose, and opened the door for me.

I entered and found Logan on the phone, as he always was. He waved me to a seat, and I took a comfortable club chair by the floor to ceiling windows. I looked down at the street hundreds of feet below. I wondered if I would have been tempted to leap out if the window could be opened. Logan continued to talk for a few more minutes. Normally, I would have been interested to hear what he was saying, but now I just tuned him out. Finally, he hung up the phone and came over. He took the chair facing me.

"Jim, I've known you for almost thirty years. We started at the bank within months of each other. You're the smartest man I know."

I said nothing but just sat there, waiting for him to go on. He tapped the folder on his lap.

"What the fuck is going on, Jim? If even half of what is in this dossier is true, you're a pervert."

"What's in there?"

"Documents that Dolores has given her lawyers for her divorce case with you. Statements from Julia Pierce. Dolores told me much more when she came to see me, and I've also had conversations with Julia here in London."

"You've talked to Julia?"

"She claims when she stayed in your condo during her first months at the bank, you forced her to have sex with you. And that she continued to have sex with you because you told her you would fire her if she didn't."

"That's not true!" I exclaimed spontaneously.

"Jim, in light of what Dolores told me in our face to face meeting, I'm inclined to believe Julia. Your wife caught you having sex with a child prostitute here in London a couple months ago. She's sure the girl's ID was fake. She knows teenagers, and she's convinced the girl was about fifteen years old."

I followed Bud's advice, and kept silent. There was a knock on the door.

"Come in!" Logan called.

It was Julia. She was dressed professionally in her trademark designer suit and white chiffon blouse, and she wore the white-gold snake choker necklace with the red ruby eyes. Her jacket hung open, and the top two buttons of her blouse were undone. She'd exposed all of her tight cleavage, as well as the red bow at the bridge of her black bra.

She was clearly surprised to see me and gathered her blouse seams together with one hand to cover her bra.

"Oh, sorry!" she said. "I didn't know you were in a meeting, Logan. I'll come back later."

"No, no, come on in, Julia," said Logan. "I've just been telling Jim what you told me this morning. I know it's painful for you, but as you said, it's better to confront it squarely and put it behind you. I think you deserve to be here and see justice done."

"If you think so," said Julia. "I only want to do what's right for the bank."

"Yes, yes," said Logan. "Everything you've done has been for the good of the bank. You've endured enormous pain in order to maintain the bank's reputation. But in the end, it does no good to shield a sexual predator. We've got to cut the cancer out of the system."

"Yes," said Julia, her voice faltering. "I see that now."

She walked up to Logan's side, taking her hand off the seams of her blouse, letting them part again. Logan put his arm around her waist possessively, and she leaned on him. *Logan must have had sex with her this morning in his hotel*, I thought. The irony seared me like a branding iron.

"Jim, you preyed on Julia when she was vulnerable, living in your house. You've acted in a despicable manner, using your power at the bank to obtain sex from a junior employee. All this is in addition to consorting with a prostitute here in London."

He paused to see if I would respond. When I did not, he went on.

"I'm relieving you of your duties with immediate effect. You're fired, Jim. You know the drill—thirty minutes to clear out your office. Security will escort you out of the building."

I looked at Julia. She looked smug on Logan's arm. She had used me to get a plum assignment and favor her with valuable trades and contacts. She had masterfully made me the villain and herself the victim. I felt more like a fool than a villain and her victimhood was, at best, overdone. But Dolores's dossier made her story irrefutable.

I stood up. There did not seem to be anything to say, so I let myself out. They were waiting till I shut the door, so I pulled it almost all the way shut. I couldn't resist reopening it slightly and peeking through. Their eyes were for each other, and neither noticed the door. Logan's hand around Julia's waist traveled up and cupped her right breast. He leaned down, and she looked up at him. They shared a fleshy kiss. There was nothing subtle about it.

* * *

24

I closed the door softly and walked to my office to clear out my belongings. There was a man from security waiting for me there. He gave me a cardboard box, and I put my few personal effects into it. The most important was my personal laptop. He checked it to make sure it was not a bank issued one. He escorted me as I took the elevator down. He looked at me questioningly as I pressed a lower floor instead of the lobby.

"Just want to look in on HR before I leave," I said. "I'd like to check on my severance."

"As long as it's within the thirty minute window, sir," he said.

I nodded, and he followed me to HR. He waited outside the HR director's office as I went in, hurrying past the personal assistant before she could stop me. The HR director was a stern-faced woman about my age with iron gray hair. She was reading something on her large screen desktop. She dropped her reading glasses on her desk and looked up at me, though she was not surprised.

"You're here to discuss your severance, I assume, Mr. Hancock," she said.

"Yes," I said.

"Three months' salary," she said. "Your retirement account and stock options have been frozen by your wife's lawyers pending your divorce settlement. That is between you and them."

"I have nowhere to stay back in the States," I said. "My residences there are also locked down, pending the settlement. I'd like to request permission to stay on in the flat at Canary Wharf for the time being."

She tapped on her keyboard from a few minutes and ran her cursor over the screen, clicking her mouse pad for a few moments. She read the screen she had brought up.

"We don't have anyone moving in there," she said. "And we have to pay for the service contract to maintain it, whether anyone is in there or not. I suppose there is no harm in your staying there through the period of your severance. I'll give you another month to put your effects together and move out—four months in all. But you are no longer an employee of the bank. We are not liable for anything you do there during this period."

"I understand," I said. "Thank you."

Three months' salary, I thought, riding down to the lobby with the security man. *If I'm frugal, I can make it last for some time.*

*   *   *

25

I called Chad as soon as I got back to the flat at Canary Wharf. We talked about inane things for a few moments, the state of the market opening, the day's financial news. Then I brought up what I was really calling about.

"I'm a free man, Chad," I said, trying to sound bright. "You've always said you wanted to talk to me about running your bond business. I'm ready to talk now."

There was silence on the line. I waited, my fingers tightening around the handset.

"Dolores met Mack back in the States yesterday, Jim," Chad said finally. His older brother Mackenzie "Mack" Bain was the CEO of Bain Jennings. "She gave him a dossier. And she talked to him for over an hour. It wasn't pretty, Jim."

I did not say anything but waited with a sinking feeling in the pit of my stomach.

"We can't touch you, Jim. Dolores has made the rounds. I'm telling you this as a friend. I don't think anyone on Wall Street or in the City will take your calls right now. If I were you, I would spare myself the embarrassment."

I thought for few moments, hoping he wouldn't hang up on me.

"You think there's anyone who would talk to me now?"

"The Chinese are sensitive to image and face," he said. "I don't think they'd be willing to talk to you. But the Russians, they usually don't care about sex stuff."

"Money laundering," I said. "You think that's my only option now?"

"It sounds harsh, I know. But I'm just trying to be honest here."

"Chad," I tried to keep the desperate note out of my voice, "you don't have to hire me. Take me on as a consultant, just an anonymous month-to-month contract. You've got dozens of people like that. I don't want much money, just something to pay for room and board and keep myself busy."

"I'd love to do that, Jim. I know you could make a lot of money for me here in London. But Mack was very clear—no relationship of any kind. Nothings stays secret, you know that. We just can't afford the reputational risk. Our reputation is our most valuable asset."

Dolores wanted to be rid of me. She wanted all our assets, but why was she hell-bent on destroying me? I just could not understand the depth of her hatred. It was like catching me in bed with Roxy had stirred something dark and primeval within her.

*   *   *

26

I texted Roxy about it, but there was no response from her till the next day. She came over to Canary Wharf for dinner. I'd spent several hours making a fairly elaborate Italian meal. She said nothing about the elegant table setting, the candles, or the meal. She sat at the table, playing with her pasta with a fork and sipping her Pellegrino with the lime slice in it. She was not very sympathetic.

"You just let them sack you?" she asked. "You didn't think about using their relationship as a weapon to fight back?"

"I thought about that, Roxy. But it wouldn't be much of a weapon. Julia doesn't report to Logan. Their relationship is inappropriate, and technically, it's against the rules, but people have affairs at work all the time. I'm pretty sure he hasn't actually given her any material benefits yet. Whereas there is hard evidence that I steered trades to her team."

"You could get a detective agency to find evidence of their relationship. You could at least ruin her marriage. And maybe his as well."

"What good would that do me?"

Roxy did not reply, but her expression did not soften. She stood up from the table, leaving most of her food uneaten. She took my hand and led me to the bedroom. We had sex unlike any we had had thus far in our relationship. She rode me hard but showed little consideration, seemingly bent on nothing but her own pleasure. Her focus on herself and her lack of interest in me deadened my excitement. I felt no ascent toward climax. She raked my shoulders with her nails. But I remained dry.

"What's the matter, Mr. Hancock?" she asked afterward. "Don't I excite you anymore?"

"What really excited me when we made love was the thought that you cared about me, Roxy. I hope I gave you what you wanted."

"You did well for an old man," she said, getting out of the bed with her usual feline grace. "I think I'm going to spend the night at home. I've got an early start tomorrow."

*   *   *

27

It was hard for me to get used to doing nothing. I woke up in the morning, went through the financial news as I always did, and ideas crowded my brain. It always took me a few moments to remember that I had nowhere to implement them. I began to text Roxy to give her my ideas. She always texted back immediately, and we often had involved online discussions.

These were now the most intense interactions we had, for I rarely saw her in person. She was very busy and had no time to come all the way to Canary Wharf. When I volunteered to come to her place in West London, she usually demurred, saying that she was too tired. When I did go over, I tried to bring a meal, some choice delicacies, things I knew that she liked. But she had no appetite and little appreciation. I had to constantly remind myself of how young she was, and that this self-absorption was normal.

Another month went by, and at the end of it, things took a turn for the better. She was eleven weeks into her pregnancy, and her morning sickness tapered off. She began to show, and we went shopping for maternity clothes. Her pale skin took on a lustrous sheen, the glow associated with pregnancy, and her eyes were even brighter. She grew much more cheerful. We began meeting every day again. She became more amorous and kept me up most of the night. She acted like she cared about me again, and this made me desire her all the more.

Our visits to the maternity clinic were a lot more pleasant now. She delighted in watching the baby's rapid heartbeat and was excited about watching it move on the ultrasound. At her twelve-week checkup, the technician gave us the ultrasound printout saying, "You can start picking out pink outfits. It's a girl. She gave us a pretty good view today."

Roxy began spending more time at my flat in Canary Wharf, and her clothes and shoes began filling up the empty closet space. She often brought Alfie over, leaving him with me when she went to work. The big Great Dane and I soon became good friends. He accompanied me on my riverside walks and slow runs and sat at my feet obediently at sidewalk coffee shops. My rebroken ribs were still very sore, but I felt better every day.

Roxy's motorbike remained parked in her garage now. We took taxis everywhere together, sampling interesting ethnic restaurants and hip clubs. Roxy had an encyclopedic knowledge of the London scene. Several times she was approached by people asking her about Nick, and she always responded, "Nick and I aren't together anymore." I felt a spark of anticipation whenever she said that, for I always hoped that she was continue and say, "This is James. I'm with him now." But she never did and never introduced me to these people. When I asked her why, she said, "They're not the sort of people you want to know, Mr. Hancock."

I became used to my more relaxed schedule. I still felt engaged with work, for Roxy and I communicated throughout the day, often spending hours discussing complex scenarios. We were literally working together at Bain Jennings. We grew to be mentally in sync and could finish each other's sentences. Her performance grew even better, and she got a fat month-end extraordinary bonus.

She came to the flat that evening, beaming. I hugged her in the entrance hallway, and she gave me the envelope with the deposit advice without a word. I looked at the amount and realized that it was the first time she had been paid such a large sum. So I let my mouth drop open, as though I was shocked.

"My god, Roxy!" I exclaimed. "This is unbelievable! You're the best!"

"Let's go out, Mr. Hancock," she said. "We've got a lot to celebrate."

"Of course," I said. "It's a big bonus."

"I've made a reservation at Langan's."

"Why Langan's? It's rather staid."

"It was where you took me on our first night out together."

We went to Langan's, and the maître d' nodded at me before conducting us to a choice table. The sommelier recognized Roxy's shape and condition and brought a list of mocktails. I decided to keep her company, and we ordered two virgin margaritas. Roxy and I went over her work of the past week, analyzing our decisions and trying to see where we could have done better in light of the realized outcomes. Halfway through her steak, she sat back and sighed contentedly.

"I'm having so much fun working with you, Mr. Hancock. I wish there was a way we could find a place to work together officially. We're such a great team."

"Chad won't hire me, Roxy. No one will. I've been working the phone. I can't even get anyone to take my calls."

"This will blow over, won't it?"

"Probably not. In this age of #metoo, everyone is gun shy. I'm just too much of a risk."

She worked on the rest of her steak with a thoughtful expression her face.

"Chad wants to transfer me to the States," she said when she was done. She waited while the waiter cleared away our main course plates and took our dessert orders. "Will you come with me?"

"I have to move out of the flat at Canary Wharf at the end of the month," I said. "I've nothing to keep me in London. I just got the last paycheck of my severance. I might as well go back to the States and hope that Bud can save my condo in the city."

She reached forward and put her hand on my wrist.

"We're partners, Mr. Hancock. I couldn't have got this bonus without you. Half of it is yours."

I put my other hand on top of hers.

"It's all yours, Roxy. Your name is on every trade. You took all the risk."

"We can keep working together in the States. Just like we are now. And in a year or so, we can strike out on our own."

"A boutique advisory," I said slowly.

"Exactly. There are more than a dozen of them working for us at Bain Jennings. Many of them are based in the States. It's fee income, but they do pretty well. If we continue to post results like we've just done, we'll be able to build an A-list client base."

"I don't think a lot of people will give me business," I said, coming down to earth again. "They'd have to disclose my name if I was a principal."

"We'll make something work," said Roxy. She rubbed the small swell at her belly. "We'll soon have another mouth to feed."

I leaned forward, ran my fingers through her silky hair, and kissed her.

"I want to be with you, Roxy Reid," I said. "Always."

It came out spontaneously before I could stop myself. For now, I was sure that I was in love. It was a deep, tearing, disruptive experience that I had never known before. I wanted to tell her how my heart beat faster every time she was near, how every minute away from her was torture, how she filled my thoughts when I was awake and my dreams when I was asleep, how her smile lit up my day, and her laughter thrilled my senses. But I knew it was impossible, ridiculous, so I said none of these things.

I waited with bated breath. I was hoping, yearning for her to reciprocate. She smiled at me, but I could not read the look in her eyes. Was she happy? Was she amused? Was she scornful?

"Would you like some coffee, Mr. Hancock?" she asked. "Or some port?"

CHAPTER 3

APOTHEOSIS

Narrator: Roxy

1

A week after I took Mr. Hancock to dinner at Langan's, Saira called me, sounding unusually excited. It took a lot to excite Saira, so my ears pricked up. She made some inane chitchat before getting to the main reason for her call.

"My parents have been to see Iftekhar's parents," she said. "They've had several meetings. But last week, they proposed me as a bride and daughter-in-law. The Salims have accepted!"

"No way!" I said, passing my hand over my stomach—I still had not gotten used to my distending shape.

"Yes! The engagement is in a fortnight." She paused and then went on in a rush. "This would never have happened without you, Roxy. And I owe Hancock a lot. The Salims would never have seen me without his intercession."

"I did it for Nick, Saira, you know that. You and I, we stopped the stupid war between our menfolk. But I'm happy it's turned out well for you."

"That's an understatement," she said. She paused again before going on. "Roxy, I want you and Hancock to attend the engagement."

"Are you sure you want me there, Saira? Your family and especially your brother may not be too pleased to see me."

"Stuff them," she said. "You're my best friend. I've got a formal invitation card that I want to give you. Where are you this evening?"

"I'll be at Mr. Hancock's flat in Canary Wharf. I'll text you the address. I should be there by eight."

Saira arrived at a quarter past eight, dressed to the nines. She wore a gold brocaded sari, a heavy gold necklace, gold bangles, and diamond earrings. Her hair was in an intricate coiffure that was obviously not done at home.

"I was shopping with Iftekhar's mother," she said, slightly self-conscious. "She fancies all this gold jewelry. It's not really my cup of tea."

"You look great," I said dutifully, though I thought it looked a bit garish.

"Lovely indeed," echoed Mr. Hancock.

She came in and sat down in the living room. I offered her tea, but she declined, saying she had just had some.

"Roxy, are you pregnant?" she asked with a pointed look at my shape, a note of surprise in her voice.

"Yes," I said. "Yes, I am."

"How far gone?"

"About three months," I said.

"Is it Nick's?"

"No," I said.

She waited for me to elaborate, but I did not say anything further. She was obviously curious, and her eyes went from my belly to

Mr. Hancock questioningly. I did not answer her mute question. I was not sure what I would tell her if she asked me explicitly. She did not ask, and the moment passed.

She took a big cream envelope out of her purse, and handed it to me. "Roxy Reid and James Hancock" was inscribed on it in a flowing calligraphic hand. I took it and sat back down again by Mr. Hancock. I read through the flowery print on the invitation card and passed it to Mr. Hancock. She told us about the wedding that was to be in six months' time and extracted a promise from us to attend that as well. The conversation flagged after that, but I could see from the way she lingered that she had something more that she wanted to talk about. Ever the perfect gentleman, Mr. Hancock saw that she was inhibited by his presence.

"Why don't you show Saira the balcony," he suggested. "The view of the City skyline is quite impressive."

She accepted with an eagerness that confirmed my perception. Mr. Hancock remained inside, while Saira and I walked out through the French windows. The balcony wrapped around the entire flat, two sides of the building and really afforded some of the best views of the City. Saira wrapped herself in the *pallu* of her heavy brocaded sari against the chill. She admired the view with unfeigned wonder. Out of sight of Mr. Hancock, she put her arms around me and hugged me.

"Roxy, I've known you all my life," she said, her arm still around my shoulder. "You know how much my family love me, and I love them. But they don't know me like you do."

"Yes," I agreed.

"They were really pressuring me to marry Yusuf, and nothing I said made a difference. No matter how many times I said he's a wally, their answer was always the same, 'You'll grow to love him.'" I squeezed her hand on my shoulder, and she smiled. "He's finally recovering from the beating you gave him, by the way. But I hear that everyone is making fun of him for being thumped by a girl."

"I'm just happy you didn't have to marry him, Saira."

"Neither my family nor Mr. Hancock would ever understand, Roxy, but you do. It's not about the Salims' money, for I'm already spoiled rotten. My family buy me anything I ask for." She took a deep breath and said with heartfelt joy, "But I've *escaped!*"

Then she gestured around with her free hand at the view and the palatial flat behind us. She kissed me on the cheek. "And so have you!"

"Yes," I said slowly. "I have. And I'm never going back."

* * *

2

The two weeks till the engagement ceremony passed quickly. I had pretty much moved into Mr. Hancock's Canary Wharf flat with Alfie. The days were filled with exciting work, stimulating interactions with Mr. Hancock on the phone, by text, and by email. The nights were filled with interactions of a different kind, for pregnancy pushed my normally healthy sexual appetite into overdrive. I constantly wanted to be stimulated, and he tried his best to give me all that I wanted. I often woke him in the middle of the night, and even groggy from sleep, he always took delight in physically bonding with me.

Saira's engagement was on a Saturday afternoon in a rented hall in Tower Hamlets. It was a relatively short taxi ride from Canary Wharf. We were not sure about the etiquette for the ceremony, so we decided to take no chances and arrive quite early. Saira's brother Hamid was on the outer steps, talking on his phone. He had a few young men around him. They were all dressed in formal silk shalwar kameez. It looked rather quiet.

"I guess we're too early," I said.

"Well, better early than late," said Mr. Hancock, smiling.

We got out of the taxi, and I looked up and down the street. It was a side street, and we were the only white people that I could see. I called Saira, and she picked up immediately.

"We're just outside," I said. "Should we come in?"

"Yes, come on in! I've told Hamid to expect you. He should be out there with several of my cousins."

Reassured, we walked up the steps, and Mr. Hancock greeted Hamid.

"Congratulations, Mr. Khan," he said. "This is a happy day, isn't it?"

Hamid nodded, acknowledging Mr. Hancock without saying anything. My attention was focused on him, for he did not look at all happy to see me. Then I felt a sudden sharp shot of pain in my left shoulder, and I was pushed forward sharply.

"Hey!" I said angrily as I stumbled on a step and nearly fell.

I heard scuffling behind me.

"Run, Roxy!" Mr. Hancock shouted. "Run now!"

I regained my balance and turned around to see Mr. Hancock struggling with Saira's cousin Yusuf—the same Yusuf that I had pounded months earlier at Forty-forty. I put my hand behind the left shoulder of my dress and felt the sticky wetness of welling blood. Then I saw the long knife in Yusuf's hand and realized that while he had given me a superficial gash, Mr. Hancock's intervention had prevented him from stabbing me to death.

"It's none of your bloody business, you motherfucking *gora*!" yelled Yusuf. "Get the fuck out of my way!"

"Get out of here, Roxy!" Mr. Hancock shouted again. "Go—"

His voice was cut short as Yusuf wrenched his right arm free and stabbed him in the gut. He twisted the knife and pulled it out. Mr. Hancock grunted with pain, but he would not relinquish his hold on Yusuf's left hand.

"Stop him, you assholes!" I screamed at Hamid and his men.

But they were all melting away. I realized that they wanted nothing to do with the police and would deny that they had been present. I fumbled in my purse, cursing, but even as I hurried, Yusuf stabbed Mr. Hancock again this time higher up, under his breastbone.

"Save yourself, Roxy…please," Mr. Hancock's voice was a dry wheeze, but he still held on to Yusuf.

I finally found my switchblade and scrambled down the steps on my stupid high heels. Coming up behind Yusuf, I put my hand on his shoulder. He realized his danger and tried to turn his knife on me, but Mr. Hancock still held him fast. I stabbed Yusuf under his left shoulder blade, driving the shaft of the weapon all the way to hilt, exactly as Nick had taught me. It was a death blow to the heart, and as soon as I pulled the blade out, Yusuf collapsed. He fell backward past me and rolled down the steps onto the pavement.

Mr. Hancock lay on his back on the steps, the midsection of his white shirt a mass of blood. I went down by him, my knees cushioned by the folds of my dress. I took his head in my lap.

"Are you okay?" panted Mr. Hancock.

"I'm fine," I said, wooden faced. "Hang in there, I'm calling an ambulance."

I called 999 and gave the dispatcher our location. Hamid and his men had vanished, and the street had emptied of people. I felt I was alone in the world with Mr. Hancock and Yusuf's body on the pavement.

"Roxy," rasped Mr. Hancock. "If I die, I want you to know—"

"You're not going to die!" I snapped. "Save your strength. You're going to need it." Then I softened my tone. "The ambulance will be here soon."

He did not reply but continued to look at me. *His eyes are gray,* I thought. *Such a pale gray. I never noticed that before.* He moved his arm, and his hand found mine, his face straining with the effort. He gave my hand a weak squeeze, and I squeezed back. For some reason, it made me think of the way he had held me on the dancefloor at the Argentinian restaurant. That memory brought others to mind— laughing together in the antique four-poster bed at the Taylor Hotel, jazz dancing at Forty-forty, nights of passion in the flat at Canary Wharf.

His expression was tender—with a start I realized that it was the way he always looked at me. The realization of how much I had taken him for granted dawned slowly, like thick treacle being poured out of a bottle. It sparked a twinge of guilt that grew rapidly. I recalled the many times I had repaid his kindness and thoughtfulness with indifference and sometimes even with nastiness. *He signed away his fortune to keep me out of court and protect my honor,* I thought. *And I didn't even give him a word of thanks, let alone sympathize with his despair.*

My lip quivered, and I said, "I'm sorry I wasn't nicer to you, Mr. Hancock. I've been a bitch. It's just what I am."

"Don't say that, Roxy," he whispered, trying to squeeze my hand again. "You've given me more than I can ever repay."

He smiled, and I smiled back at him. I didn't know what to do so I prayed, feeling slightly foolish. *I've never asked you for anything, Lord,* I bargained. *But if you let him live, I'll turn over a new leaf. I'll do your bidding. I'll work with the poor. I'll help the weak. Just give me the chance to be good to him.*

It took another three or four minutes for the first emergency vehicle to arrive. It was a police car with a pair of young coppers, a white man and a South Asian woman. The woman came to help me with a first aid kit from the police car. She was cutting away Mr. Hancock's shirt when the ambulance arrived.

Even as the paramedics leaped from their vehicle, I could see Mr. Hancock's breathing getting shallower. The paramedics asked me to move aside and took over. They worked on him for another half an hour, but I already knew what they were going to tell me.

"I'm sorry miss," one of them said to me. "Your friend didn't make it."

"Please close his eyes," I said, struggling to form words. "Don't leave him staring at the sky like that."

"We'll need a statement, miss," said the South Asian policewoman.

*　*　*

3

Mr. Hancock was not perfect. He was often a slave to his passions. He was no worse than most men, but he flagellated himself for these failings. Unlike most people, he always *tried* to do the right thing, to do his duty as he saw it. He tried so very hard! In the end, he died doing what he thought was right—saving me.

Did I love him? I honestly don't know. When I held him with his blood leaking out and staining my dress, his life dribbling out of him, I thought I would never be able to breathe again. My throat was so tight that I thought I would suffocate and die right there with him. Choked up as I was, my eyes remained dry. The tears would not come.

I really have no memory of the days that followed. I went back to his flat in Canary Wharf and wandered around in it aimlessly. I don't know if I ate, drank, or bathed. Alfie knew that something was very wrong and followed me around, whining for attention. I did not feel like petting him, though I guess I must have fed him. Nick called me incessantly, left texts and voice mails; Saira called a few times as well. But I did not respond to either of them. I got one text from Chad Bain, "Take your time. Come back when you're ready."

I don't know how many days I stayed at the flat at Canary Wharf, but I knew that I could not stay there forever. Eventually, I packed my things into a couple of cases and prepared to move back to my place in West London. I was doing a sweep of his big desk to make sure I had not left anything there when I came across a white envelope with just the letter *R* on it. It was in Mr. Hancock's neat flowing handwriting, and it looked incomplete, for there seemed to be half an *o* just after it. It was unsealed, and there was a single sheet of heavy bond paper in it. I unfolded it with trembling fingers. It was a note in Mr. Hancock's handwriting, and it was undated.

My dearest Roxy,

I am writing this for myself, as I know that I will never have the courage to give it to you. It is so simple and yet so complex, so obvious, and yet so impossible to explain, even to you, let alone to anyone else. So I'll just say it—I love you, Roxy. I love you more than life itself.

I bared my heart to you that night at Langan's, and it was kind of you not to refuse me outright. I know you deserve so much better. I have no money, no prospects, and my youth is long gone. I meant what I said to you the day we met—you're a goddess. I have nothing to offer a girl like you.

So rather than asking for your hand, I will simply tell you my wishes, my hopes, and my dreams. I wish I were thirty years younger so that I could at least see your beauty through the eyes of a young man. I hope that when our time together is done, you will look back on it with compassion and forgive my sordid weaknesses. And I dream that our daughter will grow up to become a goddess like her mother.

I wish that I had something tangible to give you. But fate has left me with nothing of value. I have put my high school class ring on a silver chain. It is a worthless trinket, but perhaps one day, I will offer it to you and hope that you will not laugh at it.

It has been a wild ride, Roxy. We both know that it must end, for the two of us are an impossible pairing. You are a ray of sunshine, a light in the darkness, a bringer of joy and love and life. Bless you, Roxy Reid.

James Hancock

There was an old silver signet ring on a new silver chain in the envelope. I ran my fingers over the face of the ring, the motifs of a flaming torch and a pair of oxen. I read the year of his graduation and the name of his high school in Nebraska. I heard rather than saw the spatter of a tear on the heavy paper. I quickly put the sheet down on the desk again and wiped my eyes. But the tears, bottled up for so long, would not stop. I ran rather than walked to the bedroom and threw myself on the bed where we had made so much love. I curled up into a fetal position, my hands on my swollen belly. My tears turned into noisy sobs, and my whole body shook with the outpouring of my grief. I sobbed till I could sob no more, till my throat was sore and my eyes were raw. Then I just lay there, exhausted, cauterized. I clutched his ring and held it to my cheek.

"You stole all his hard-earned money, Dolores," I whispered. "I hope it makes you happy. But I have the ring of his youth, and it's worth more to me than all the money in the world."

* * *

4

The police and the coroner's office would not turn over Mr. Hancock's body to me. They tried to turn it over to the bank, but they would not accept it. The authorities contacted Dolores, but she asked them to dispose of it in the manner of an indigent person. When I heard this, I shook with impotent rage.

Eventually, his son Nathan Hancock flew over and took charge of the body. Chad Bain put me in touch with him, and I met him at the morgue. Nathan tried to work with a funeral home in the Connecticut town where the Hancocks had lived as a family. However, he found that Dolores had talked to the town council, accusing her former husband of sexual deviancy. She had managed to get them to block all the funeral homes in the town from accepting his body. In the end, Nathan arranged to have it flown back to the small town in Nebraska where his father had grown up. He contracted with a funeral home in that town, and they arranged the logistics of transporting the body, working with the London morgue and the coroner's office.

All this took over two weeks. As Nathan knew no one in London, I felt the least I could do was to give him company. We spent time together every day, talking and walking through the parks, often with Alfie. It began as an obligation, but as the days passed, I gradually began to look forward to spending time with him. Nathan had so many stories about growing up with his father, and I was keen to hear all of them. There was so much about Mr. Hancock that I did not know, for Nebraska men are brought up to be modest. All I knew of him was through talk at the bank, where he was renowned as a tech geek, a master of the arcane mathematics of trading and portfolio management.

But Nathan told me that he was a fantastic skier, who regularly took on the toughest chutes in the Rockies, the Alps, and even Alaska. Nathan showed me helmet-cam videos of his father's descents on his phone, and they were *terrifying*!

"And you've got to remember," said Nathan, "that Dad learned to ski relatively late in life, after he made some money at the bank. My sister, Heather, and I learned to ski as children, and we're technically better skiers than he was. But for him, everything was an equation to be solved. I remember the first time we skied Corbet's Couloir together, that iconic run at Jackson Hole. He worked out everything so precisely, from drop-in angle to maximum speed, like it was a physics problem. A couple of years ago, he crashed heli-skiing in Alaska. He broke almost every bone down the right side of his body. He was in rehab for months, but a year later, he was back, skiing as hard as ever. You could knock Dad down, but he always got up again."

"Yes," I said. "He always got up again. No matter how hard he was hit."

I knew that he was a runner, but he never told me that he'd qualified for and run the New York Marathon numerous times with a best time under three hours.

"When we were children, he took us on a hike to the top of Mount Marcy in the Adirondacks. We were both under ten, and it's a really challenging hike. But I'll always remember how encouraging he was. We had such a good time that day. Dad worked all the time and traveled a lot for work, but he really tried to do things with us."

And Nathan said, he was an excellent tennis player.

"I'm not too bad myself," said Nathan. "But Dad could beat me easily. And that was another sport he picked up late in life."

"Why did he start all these things so late?" I asked.

"Dad's family was not well-off. My grandfather was a janitor, and Grandma was a housewife. Dad worked all through high school and college."

"He never told me that!" I exclaimed. "I thought he was a typical middle-class bloke."

"He didn't tell us either. He did very well at the bank right from the outset. So ever since I can remember, we were pretty affluent. It was my grandfather that told us about Dad's younger days."

"He met your mum at university. He told me."

"Mom and Dad should never have gotten married," said Nathan. "But she got pregnant senior year—with me—and Dad felt marrying her was the right thing to do. For as long as I can remember, they were never happy. Dad tried so very hard to make it work, date nights, flowers, chocolates, family holidays. He convinced himself that since he was doing all the right things, things *must* be going well. But Mom just didn't like him. Every little thing he did irritated her. She was constantly picking at him, finding fault. And it didn't help that he had to work such long hours, so we saw so little of him. Home was never a happy place for my sister and me."

"He tried all right," I said. "I saw him. But your mum, she's—"

"Difficult," Nathan said before I could finish. "I couldn't wait to leave home. I went off to college and never went back. I confess, I wasn't very good about keeping in touch with my parents."

"Yet, here you are in London," I said. "Your mother wanted him cremated like a homeless person. And some months ago, I heard your sister tell him that she wished he was dead."

"What do you mean?" asked Nathan, shocked.

I told him about Heather's call to Mr. Hancock, and his expression became grim.

"Heather always took Mom's side," he said. "I just tried to stay out of their fights. It was more like spouse abuse because Dad never fought back. I hated how he just let Mom walk all over him. I swore I would never be a wimp like that."

"He wasn't a wimp," I snapped. "He was a gentleman."

He patted Alfie's large head and scratched under his chin. Alfie licked him. Nathan looked so much like his father and had so many of his mannerisms, that sitting and talking with him made me misty eyed. It was like Mr. Hancock was there, yet he wasn't. He ran his hand down his face, nose between thumb and forefinger, exactly as his father used to do, and I felt the tears begin to run down my face.

"What's the matter? Is it something I said?" His voice and his concern were so like Mr. Hancock's—that it just made things worse. I began to bawl, and he put his arms around me, patting me awkwardly. I slowly regained control of myself and wiped my face. He gave me his clean white linen handkerchief, and I used it, thanking him in a hoarse whisper.

"I'm sorry," I said. "I'm not normally sappy like this. I guess pregnancy is making me emotional."

He continued to hold me, and after a while, I put my arms around him. It felt good to have him holding me.

*   *   *

5

I flew back to America with Nathan, accompanying Mr. Hancock's casket to Nebraska. It was a protracted depressing journey, and I honestly don't think I would have made it without Nathan's shoulder to cry on—which I did many times. We rented a car and followed the funeral home hearse on the long cheerless drive from Omaha. We finally arrived at the small Nebraska town where Mr. Hancock had grown up. In England, we would have called it a village, for it was no more than a single rather dilapidated main street with a handful of backstreets laid out in a grid pattern. We checked into the only motel in town and dropped off our bags.

The people at the funeral home were caring and comforting, radiating Midwestern kindness. They provided all the requisite arrangements. But it was sad to see the thin turnout in the large hall at the funeral service. Nathan had published an online obituary and arranged with the funeral home to make the normal local announcements. But less than a dozen of Mr. Hancock's high school classmates showed up. Only two attendees, a middle-aged blonde woman and a balding man, stayed on after Nathan's eulogy to partake of the coffee and cake.

"He moved away right after high school," said the blonde woman. "He was really studious in school, a genius. He was always happy to help anyone with math. Even people that bullied him."

145

"He was bullied?" I asked.

"Mercilessly," she replied. "He was such a nerd, such an easy target. He just brought it on himself." She looked over at the balding man and went on. "Remember how we replaced his District Science Fair poster board with a blank sheet when he'd gone to the restroom? He came back and ran around like a chicken with its head cut off, trying to find it, begging everyone to give it back. The judges reprimanded him for taking up space without having a project. It doesn't sound that funny now. I guess you had to be there."

The blonde woman and the man both laughed. I didn't think it was funny at all, and my fists bunched. I kept my face straight with an effort.

"He won the district cross country race in his senior year," said the balding man, chuckling. "But afterward, the team still gave him a wedgie in the locker room."

"What's that?" I asked.

"Pulled his underwear up his ass," said the man, his chuckles turning into laughter. The blonde woman joined in, but then she stopped, looking self-conscious.

"We really mustn't laugh at him now," she said, becoming serious with an obvious effort. "This is not the right time or place." She turned to me. "How did you know him?"

"I worked with him in London," I said.

"I hope he learned to be one of the boys over there," said the balding man.

"No, he didn't," I said. "He never learned to be an asshole."

Both of them looked at me with shocked expressions, as though they could not believe anyone could be so ill bred.

"Just goes to show you," said the blonde woman with a sniff. "They said he was a very successful banker who made all kinds of money, but look around, he didn't have many friends, did he?"

"He must have led a lonely life," said the balding man as they both turned to leave.

A few minutes later, I was alone with Nathan and one of the assistants from the funeral home.

"Do you still want a graveside service?" the assistant asked.

"Yes," said Nathan. "I'll come out. Roxy, you can wait in here if you like."

"No, no," I said. "I'll come out with you."

London seemed to have followed us to Nebraska, for it was raining outside. The funeral director did the traditional reading, and the gravediggers lowered the casket into the ground. I put my ceremonial handful of earth into the grave and watched it patter on the casket.

I wanted so much more for him—a ceremony commensurate with the man he was, a celebration of his genius, his achievements, his humanity. Instead, he lay in a decaying town on a windblown featureless landscape among people who had tormented him. Looking around, I could see the horizon in all directions across the flat plain. I clutched his ring that now hung on the silver chain around my neck. I rubbed my belly and felt the child I carried within me, the comingling of his essence with mine. The child he would never see. I started to cry again.

"It's not fair," I said, weeping. "It's just not fair."

Nathan put his arms around me, and his embrace was so like his father's that it made me cry harder.

ABOUT THE AUTHOR

R. M. Burgess grew up in Madison, Wisconsin, but following itinerant parental careers, was educated in India and England before completing graduate work at Cornell. As a successful professional researcher, Burgess writes academic articles for a living but is passionate about fiction. Burgess published four fantasy novels in the New Eartha series before making this attempt at a contemporary romance novel.

A licensed bike racer, marathon runner, sometime triathlete, keen skier and world traveler, Burgess currently resides in Philadelphia.

CPSIA information can be obtained
at www.ICGtesting.com
Printed in the USA
LVHW111550201019
634739LV00002B/318/P